THE LIFE AND TIMES

OF A TEABOY

By the same author

The Meat Eaters (in Phoenix Paperback)

The

LIFE AND TIMES

of a

TEABOY

———

Michael Collins

PHOENIX HOUSE

London

First published in Great Britain 1994

© 1994 Michael Collins

Phoenix House, Orion House,
5 Upper St Martin's Lane,
London WC2H 9EA

Michael Collins has asserted his right
under the Copyright, Designs and Patents Act 1988
to be identified as the author of this work

A CIP catalogue record for this book
is available from the British Library

ISBN 1 89758 031 2 (cased)
ISBN 1 89758 076 2 (paperback)

Typeset at The Spartan Press Ltd,
Lymington, Hants
Printed in Great Britain by Butler & Tanner Ltd,
Frome and London

Dedicated to my parents and my wife

Acknowledgements to

Maggie McKernan
David Chalfant
Professor Augustine Martin UCD
Professor Seamus Deane UCD
Dennis O'Driscoll
Professor William O'Rourke
Linda Williams
Alfred Roach
Richard Napora
Spike and Wicklow

THE BIRTH

Christmas didn't just come; it had to be planned or it would be a disaster. Feeney knew all about preparation. His mind was always on the future. He had a saying, Today is the future. In February he purchased a cow which he had mated immediately so that she could give birth before Christmas. He planned to sell the calf in advance of leaving its mother's udder, delivering it to its new owners in the New Year. The sale of the calf would pay for Christmas. It was a simple plan that he had learned from his people down through the years. They had been farmers, living on the bartered flesh and produce of animals. Now there were only two weeks to Christmas.

The sound of the factory horn competed with the church bells. Feeney waited for his daughter at the end of the long drive, leaning against his bicycle, dressed in a soiled long black coat. He had his right trouser leg tucked into his sock to keep it from getting tangled in the chain. Entrenched in the past, Feeney would never take to cars. The bicycle accompanied him everywhere. Even when he walked without it, he had his right hand out, perceptibly pushing the phantom. Few people had cars yet, but everyone knew Feeney would never be a man to take to them. He was one of the last of a breed of bicycling men.

His daughter came down the long school drive with her friends. The bicycle wheeled out in front of the gate, Feeney by its side. 'Maria,' Feeney said, nodding his head. The front wheel moved slightly, allied with Feeney.

The girls crowded around her, wide-eyed, staring at Feeney.

Feeney stood at the gate, the bicycle poised, the eye of the lamp staring at them.

'Maria?' Feeney said again.

Maria moved from the cluster of girls and went over to him, her face flushed with embarrassment.

'It's the cow,' Feeney said, dipping his head. 'I need a hand with her.'

Maria curled her black hair behind her ear nervously. 'I've got to go back for a maths exam this afternoon.'

Feeney ran his tongue over his teeth. He had strong blue eyes. 'I'll take care of that.'

The girls stood about in their disquieting pubescence, with blotched faces, big feet and hands, the secret biology of their lives concealed beneath convent blue uniforms. 'Can you believe it?' they whispered, ashamed for her.

Feeney ignored their stares, but he heard the giggles and whispers.

Maria got up on the crossbar. Feeney took a running start for effect, swinging his right leg over the seat, mounted the bicycle, and headed down toward the town, all in one glorious piece of choreography, like in the cowboy films. The girls stood by and turned their heads, mortified at a fourteen-year-old on a crossbar.

The midday sun hung weak in a sky that threatened rain. A strong wind carried the churning clouds low over the ground as he raced against the first showers, the wings of his coat flapping. The handlebars turned onto the main street, the balanced weight of his daughter accounted for in the unconscious flex of his buttocks, the back wheel licking up a trail of dirt onto his back, the ingrained stigma of all bicycling men.

In the town the sun barely peeked over the narrow streets, cordoned off by black roofs and solid brick. The bicycle glided through the premature coldness, a mechanical shadow, sucked into cracks and then re-emerging on the walls.

A melancholy smell of lard and cabbage water hung in the air. Everything was falling apart, but it maintained a Protestant severity, the shopkeepers clinging to the incorruptible pride of being associated with the British Empire. Feeney participated in the intangibles of the place, its history and its Orangemen, getting money from the work he had done out in the fields, work these people had no interest in, or cared for. He took nothing as insult, nor did he feel inferior, only different. It was part of life in a border town.

Feeney's shadow stopped. He dismounted. 'Right then.' He brushed his coat, shuffling his shoulders. 'I'll have to get some stuff around the place. Go across to Leahy and see if he has time to stop down in a while. I'll be waiting for you over at Mrs Sweeney's. Right?'

Maria left. Feeney watched after her, seeing the red mark from the crossbar on her legs. He puffed up his cheeks. The money would be there when the cow dropped the calf. Grim satisfaction cracked his face. He'd get her a bicycle of her own for Christmas. Setting his own against the wall of a shop, he stepped down a polished step. A bell jingled on coiled wire. A purring ginger cat unwrapped itself and moved off the counter. 'Hello,' Feeney said tentatively, knocking on the glass inset in a door that led to the domestic quarters. There was no sound.

Feeney clicked his fingers impatiently but was glad of the wait. The dimness shrouded him. Things would be wild enough soon with the birth. He went over a list of things he would buy with the money.

The shop was run by a wizened old widow, as were most of the small shops, spinster sisters or doll-faced little men waiting to rise and serve, to pencil accounts into tattered notebooks. Feeney waited. It was all part of a disjunctive commercial proposition. What could he say, not that commerce wasn't all based on faith in the long run. Somehow nothing was stolen. The shivering bell called nobody. The burden of existence rested on those without. Feeney waited dutifully, the honest Catholic that he was.

Behind the counter, an army of empty milk bottles huddled in the darkness. Things were set in jars or tin containers, tea, sugar, flour, sweets, blocks of butter, wooden boxes of honey combs, a teetering poverty pivoting soundlessly on oiled springs, weighed to the ounce, two ounces of tea, an egg and a rasher for one solitary meal.

A diminutive old woman emerged from a doorway that led down to a fireplace. The cat brushed her legs and disappeared. She held a cardigan around her shoulders, smelling of sleep. 'What can I get you, Feeney?'

Feeney bought a loaf of bread and two bottles of milk in the shop. Maria came across the road. 'She was asleep again,' he said to Maria. He stuck the bottles into his front pocket, took the handlebars and headed down the street. 'Any word from Leahy?'

Maria shook her head.

'He's not in, or he won't come?' Feeney asked, although he knew the answer. He did not look at her face.

'His wife says he got nothing for the last time he helped you.'

Feeney was furious. He wanted someone to share in his triumph. 'We'll do without him.'

'Are you going to sell the cow soon?' Maria said as they walked along.

'I'm going to pack the whole lot of them in, the shagging mother and calf,' Feeney nodded, his fingers spread out like a starfish on the black bicycle seat. He turned, agitated, silently enumerating the grievances he had against the town. If he stayed long enough, its awful, trenchant fatalism would force him to acknowledge that he was born an outsider, that the world of money was beyond him. He felt at home on small plots of land. He lived amongst animals. Usually, when he got like this he carried bags of hay from one end of the town to the other, or rode his bicycle hard on the roads. Animal exertion was a form of therapy.

A strip of light cut his face. He looked up and shook himself. 'What was I saying?'

Maria looked at him.

They walked briskly. The cow wasn't well. All Feeney needed was a complication and he could lose everything. The noon meal simmered in the backs of shops, mingling with the cold. His stomach turned over toast and an egg from the early morning breakfast.

'Can we eat first?' Maria lingered outside a doorway. A family ate at a table.

'Whist a bit.' Feeney breathed hard. His lungs ached from the long days. He was realistic to the point of pessimism. If he was lucky and took some pigs to market along with the calf and mother, he could afford the bicycle and have enough left for a new litter of pigs. He calculated figures in his head, carrying out his addition and subtraction, losing numbers, beginning again and again. Surely, the dealers wouldn't be that hard on him, give him a few extra pounds for the sake of Christmas. He'd have more animals in due time, but all pigs from here on out. His lips moved as he went on. He wanted to get back to the old routine, to the things he knew about.

Throughout the years he bought all sorts of animals, pigs, hens, turkeys, preparing them for slaughter. There were some farmers who preferred not to kill their own livestock. Feeney obliged. He was good at these things. Everyone knew that Feeney had a way with animals. People were somewhat wary of a dispossessed man who took to slaughter so easily. Yet, Feeney had a fixity of expression, an earnest face propped up by a family. Everything about him said, 'Whatever I have done in my past, I will do you no harm. Trust me with your slaughter.'

For all his intimacy with animals, Feeney resolved that his children would never follow in his footsteps. He never usually let the children near the animals. He kept to himself, an ambivalence which he did not understand, but felt. For whatever the reason, God had set him among animals, and he took his lot with solemn accord. He knew about heredity from breeding animals, the crude eugenics of dog handlers playing God. In his younger years he had fought the filth and degradation of a farm life, the constant attention to animal needs, the six in the morning milking, the turning of the hay, the convolution of birthing and slaughtering. The lure of the city, the careless escape, led him through Dublin and over to Liverpool. But the money soon ran out. War loomed. It was only after marriage, that milestone of realism, that he came back to the land and his animals. The return changed him. His youth soured into a conscious asceticism. He indulged in neither drink nor smoke. Sex was an obligatory procreation, a purge of frustration. He wasn't beyond a good laugh, but marriage and children threw him into a slavish need to provide. The memory of his people sitting in their own houses, on their own land, with their own animals lurked behind his every thought. He had not only disinherited himself. He had destined his children to be landless people.

Feeney took a sidelong glance at his daughter. It was better to have her down here than his sons. They were to be city men. She could keep secrets to herself. Boys were blabberers, and God knows, if any of them fainted at the sight of a cow giving birth, what would they think of themselves? He nodded to himself, yes, she was at that age where she understood about things. Feeney had a secret awe for women.

Feeney knew he was in a bad way now. His head was at him. He turned the key in a heavy padlock and pulled back the gate. He kept the stock in a rented bit of land out the back of an old widow's place off the main street. The big yard had stabled horses and coaches before the time of trains and motor cars.

Maria moved slowly behind him, exploring the walled enclosure of beasts. She had never been in there before. The animals knew Feeney's smell and nosed around their pens, the pigs butting the wooden boards. 'Go easy, boys.' He let them sniff his hot hand. From the previous night's rounds of the hotels and guest houses, he had some potato peels and carrot scrapings left. 'Come over here, Maria. You're not scared?' Feeney manoeuvred a small pig over to Maria. 'There now, let him sniff you.' The wet snout sniffed her pale hand. Feeney kept pressure on her arm, holding it steady. 'Dad.'

'Take it easy.' Feeney got a good laugh out of her, the sly

7

coercion that could be applied to women, the steady pressure of a hand holding with sustained power, not overtly harsh, masculine. He thought back to the girls at the school. He took a bucket of peels and emptied it into the pen. 'There you are.' The pigs went frantic, burying their noses in the ground. Feeney grinned. He liked pigs best of all. His mood brightened. He revelled in the unabashed animal humour, the tight coiled tail. Seeding the ground, he made a clucking sound with his tongue, calling the chickens. His animals were quiet beasts who demanded nothing but food and shelter and a hand to sniff. The enclosed space did not distress them. It made them more at ease. When he was young, his people used to let the pigs into the kitchen near the fire at night. Pig was one of the first words he had learned as a child. In later life, when he came to know more words, he looked back on the simplicity of those domestic animal names, three letter words, dog, pig, cow, hen, cat, as though they had been named before other things had names.

'Don't be scared of them,' Feeney laughed, sensing his daughter's apprehension. 'All they are is hungry.'

Maria sat still, watching her father move among his animals. The place seemed like some wayward ark.

A big stone wall with tufts of grass growing between the cracks surrounded the yard. It harboured darkness, concealing solitude. A caved-in roof aimed splintered beams at the sky. The yard walls protected the animals from the whipping winds. Feeney went to great pains to keep the animals content and healthy. He didn't want a scene or to have to forfeit the yard. The pigs had sonorous snorts that could only be heard if one stood outside the gate and listened, and the chuck of the chickens bothered nobody. He was fine in that regard. As long as he cleaned up the manure and washed down the place with a hose, the smell was tolerable, and nobody complained. Every morning before work, he got up at six o'clock, swept the yard of its muck and waste, sprinkling sawdust in the pens.

With the pigs fed, Feeney went over to Maria. He put the bottles of milk down on the ground and took out the wrapped bread. 'You'd better eat something. We'll have a long enough time here.' He felt her hands. 'You're freezing. Do you want to go up home and get a jumper?'

Maria shook her head.

Feeney blew into his hands. 'So now you see everything. Is this the way you thought it would be?'

Maria shrugged her shoulders.

'This is what has kept us for the last few years.'

'I'm cold,' Maria whispered.

Feeney pointed around the yard. 'You see how hard it is. I brought you down here to see this so you can remember what I did for you when the time comes.'

Maria smiled obliquely.

'All right, I'll say no more.' Feeney rose. 'Listen, stay put awhile until I see that everything is all right.' He walked to the back of the yard to a shed.

The cow remained unseen. Feeney stuck his head into the hemisphere of blackness. The cow moved silently. He stepped over the runny manure, reaching with his hand to stroke the long bovine head. The huge eyes glistened, the head turned. The cold nose bristled against his hand, a line of mucus frothing when it breathed. Feeney led the cow up toward the light. He wiped its mouth with the sleeve of his coat. 'There now.' The cow's eyes roamed in its head, the skin damp and hot. Feeney trembled. The cow looked bad by his estimation.

9

Jesus, what would he do if it died on him? The cow was too big to slaughter all by himself in the yard. It would have to leave the yard alive. He wondered if he should take it up to the fields for the birth. If the cow dropped dead in the yard, he had no access to a cart to bring it out. He'd even be done out of selling the meat.

The cow seemed to sense Feeney's mood.

'Come on, you whore,' Feeney said, pulling the cow forward.

The cow resisted and almost fell over. Feeney had tied a rope between the forefoot and back foot like the knackers did to keep their horses from straying. The cow limped everywhere. Feeney finally set it in the open yard. Its monstrous form, encumbered by the smallness of the place, shifted nervously. The pigs eyed it and snorted belligerently.

Maria swallowed and pointed at the cow's leg. Feeney hunched over. The shin above the hoof of the fore leg was shaved in a deep wound. He pressed the leg gently, fingering his way up to the breast, feeling if the infection had spread. The cow pulled away from him nervously. 'Christ.' The wound glistened, pink and tender. Pus oozed out when he applied pressure around the edges of the wound. The cow lowed.

Maria flinched. 'Dad!' she shrieked, curling away.

Feeney untied the frayed rope. He felt his daughter's horror. He stood up and slapped the cow's nose. His daughter was lost to him. She saw him as cruel. What the hell could he do? The cow had gone mad a few months ago and nearly destroyed the yard. He had had to tie the legs to keep the cow from kicking out at the shed door. Feeney wanted to say this to his daughter, but all he said was, 'You go over to Leahy and get him, do you hear me?' Feeney glared at the cow.

'But he said . . . ' Maria pressed herself against the wall.

Feeney grabbed her by the arm and took her to the gate. 'Tell him the cow is sick. Go on, tell him.' Feeney went out the gate and over to a chemist's shop. He came back with antiseptic cream and dabbed the wound. 'There, you see, you've cost me another two bob.' His rough fingers worked the wound. 'You did this yourself, didn't you?'

Feeney stood up and wiped his face and then mixed a bag of animal grain in a bucket, adding water with the hose, stirring the mixture. His body sweat under the black coat as he worked away. He poured the contents into a long shallow trough. The cow lapped up the mixture, impervious to Feeney's mood. It had its hostage. The food was set before it.

At least it was eating. Feeney breathed easy. He checked the barrel side of the cow, feeling the pregnancy inside, putting his chiselled face against the warm hide. It was over-pregnant by his estimation. Christ, after all this time, he soon would be rid of the beast. He resisted the urge to hurt it. He'd never experienced such disaffection with an animal before, but cows were not like pigs. They had an almost luxurious swagger to them, and long feminine lashes, eyes that regarded him with suspicion. Except for their milk, Feeney would have no part of them. The redness of their meat indicted, red and runny, cooked so many ways, unlike the placating white of pork, served one way. After a Sunday dinner of steaming cow organs, families had to walk off the bloated decadence of hard-to-digest meat. Feeney took no part in it. He had his pigs served hard and overcooked, ungarnished, the bristle of hair singed, the rubbery fat, call it cannibalism for all it was worth, he had spoken to and loved this meat. It had eaten from his hands, now he ate it with his hands. Yes, slaughter was a necessity, eating was a necessity. He left it at that, if not revelling in its baseness, then at least acknowledging the crudeness.

When Feeney finished feeding the cow, he sat down on a smoothed stone. He looked wearily at his animals. The yard, another dimension beyond the dim street, cobbled stone out of the eighteen hundreds, the loose mortar and the big stones cut awkwardly. He imagined hot horses rubbed down for the night, the warmth of their breath and flesh mixing with heat from the blacksmith's fire. Everything lay in ruins now. The widow who owned the property had migrated to an upper floor of the old house, confined to a bed set near a window to let whatever light there was fall on her wasting body. The town lived on the ghostly memory of old money, the military pensions of deceased Protestants who left all to their brittle-boned brides. Feeney had heard that one widow was leaving five thousand pounds to a cat's home.

The pigs snorted and clamoured against the pens to get Feeney's attention. The smell of the antiseptic cream made them uneasy. 'Easy boys.' Christ, he knew he shouldn't have bought the cow. It wasn't a time to gamble.

For all his association with animals and slaughter, Feeney had reserved a regard for them. A crescent scar on his brow marked him for slaughter himself. He stared at the pigs finishing the scraps. He would never openly admit it, but part of his nerves was guilt at having to do the inevitable, coming down on a Friday evening when the town was at its wildest and opening a pig's throat into a bucket, holding the shaking body. He did it sober, because he did not want to cut himself and mess up the whole thing, but the real reason lay somewhere beyond practicality. When he slaughtered, it was always a wholesale slaughter, no survivors, each one led away by the scent of his hand to the dark corner of the shed, his thick thumb making the sign of the cross on the flat forehead. He didn't want any of them to live on in fear or remembrance of what had happened to the others. Animals have memories. With the money he made from slaughter, he bought a new stock, innocent of murder, just greedy to sniff his hand and eat his scraps. That was how he was able to keep the pigs so quiet, giving them a false sense of security, treating them more like pets than livestock. Feeney was good at deceiving animals.

The cow was the problem, witness to his massacres, to the flow of animal blood, speaking in a language of smell to the frightened pigs huddled in the pen.

Feeney ate slowly, turning the food over with his tongue. The sun dissolved on the horizon. He put the milk to his lips and drank. His kidneys were at him. He got up and urinated against the wall. The light traced its own shadow of piss.

Feeney sat down again. His scrotum turned in on itself with the cold, migrating up into his body. The cow mooed. Feeney got up and led it into the stable again.

Where the hell was Maria? Feeney walked back and forth in the yard. Feeney expected the cow to start dropping the calf right there. He'd come so far for this. It was greed and stubborn pride that had put him up to it. If he'd left well enough alone, everything would have continued as it was. He knew from the start that cows were temperamental beasts. They needed an amount of grass and hay which was difficult to manage by bicycle. It had been a long year. He felt the ebb of sleep, the drifting in and out of consciousness that had become so much of a habit over the last year. He had worn himself out in the first weeks, trying to buy feed for the cow. But nothing would sustain its appetite. He finally set on taking it out after dark, up to the hill, and letting it eat on the green out back of the Gaelic pitches where the knackers' work horses grazed. The only problem was that he had to stay with the animal. He couldn't trust the knackers. On clear or rainy nights, he would lead the cow off, and find himself a tree stump. The cow didn't react well to the night feeding. Its nature tended toward day feeding and a long night ruminating. It took Feeney all his time to break the instinct in the animal. He stopped short of getting down on his hands and knees and eating with the cow under the moonlight. He was well capable of that kind of earnest lunacy. He had a family to feed and another child on the way.

Maria came into the yard. The lights in the houses were on already. 'Don't let the pigs out,' Feeney shouted. Two pigs nudged Maria, trying to push through the gate. Feeney got up and slapped the pink skin, making the pigs squeal and trot back to their pens. 'Well?' Feeney said.

Maria looked at the ground.

'I'll remember him. Well, you'll have to hold the light for me then. It's over there. Get it.'

Feeney went to the cow again. Maria followed him. He felt the fat stomach, letting his fingers work around the hind, lifting up the tail, feeling for the first signs of water. The cow pulled away and lumbered to the security of its dark quarters. Its back legs were already parted. Feeney grinned, feeling the reproach. She couldn't prevent nature from taking its course. He'd have the calf from her. He rubbed the silky mucus thread on his coat.

Feeney filled a bucket of water. 'She's nearly there.' He went out and secured the pigs, talking to them.

Maria peered at him through the slashes in the shed door. He was laughing and rubbing them. He came back and sat down in silence.

The evening died into a blustery night. Sound drifted into the yard, plates being scraped in the backyard. Tea time was over. The cow moved anxiously, lowing, coming forward in the stable, nudging Feeney. He stared at it.

'Maybe she's ready now,' Maria whispered.

Feeney put a finger to his lips. 'Shoo. Let her get comfortable first. They have their own way of preparing.' Feeney's forehead wrinkled. 'Have the light ready.'

Maria had her hands around her shoulders.

The cow bellowed plaintively. Feeney rose. 'That's it, you whore.' He took the cold bucket of water. The cow faced the wall, its hind legs far apart, like a big woman in high heels, the hooves scraping the concrete floor, trying to keep balance. The tail hung to the side of its rump. The margin of wetness spread down to the thighs. Feeney put his hands under his hot armpits to warm them before touching the cow. It mooed softly in resignation, the tremor of its legs holding it up above the damp hay. Feeney stared with the sobriety of a vet. He had done this sort of thing before. The shed filled up with hot animal breath.

'You stand over there,' Feeney whispered. 'Light the lamp.' He took his coat off and rolled up his sleeves. He blew on his hands once more to make sure they were warm.

Maria shivered in the corner. She lit the lamp and put it on the ground. She looked at the dark figure of her father leaning into the hind of the cow as though he were trying to climb into it. She closed her eyes.

Feeney eased his hand into the soft suctioning warmth of the passage. The cow's legs nearly buckled. He supported them with his shoulder, his face inches from the dark folds of flesh.

'That's it.' His wrist pivoted, his fingers crawling along the creature's inside. He felt the slime of the sack. He drew his hand out into the coldness, hot and glazed, dipping it into the bucket of water. The cold shocked him. A dribble of urine ran down his leg. 'Get more water,' he whispered to Maria.

Maria had her hands to her face. Feeney could barely make her out. 'Get me more water,' he shouted. 'Come on.' She was sobbing. She went out and came back with more water.

The cow was almost squatting, the contraction of the tunnel pushing the calf along. 'Leave it there,' Feeney said, putting out his hand to Maria. She jumped back in terror.

'Jasus,' Feeney muttered. He went around to the head, letting the cow touch his hand, the tongue instinctively licking the scent of her own insides. She shifted forward and moaned. Feeney stroked the stomach, appeased at last. The cow settled for a few long minutes, breathing hard, her hind opening slowly. A terrible smell filled the shed.

The calf dropped into a bed of straw, a sack of mucus. Feeney spooled the dark entrails. The cow turned and pushed him with its head. The calf lay inert, like a small child curled up. Feeney panicked and pushed the cow's head away. It began to moo, butting Feeney. He fell to the side, scrambling on his knees to the calf. The limbs were stiff. 'Jasus, no!' He moved away to the corner, his hand to his mouth, his tongue hanging out of his head. The cow leaned over the calf, nudging it, trying to bring it to its feet. He stared at the pit of cow's hole, then turned off the lamp.

A few minutes passed. His teeth chattered. The cow stood motionless over the dead calf, invisible. Feeney lit the lamp again. The cow's face was smeared with blood. 'Go home,' Feeney said.

'Will it be all right?'

Feeney pushed her gently. 'Go on.' Maria stood up and looked at the dead calf and then at the cow and back to her father. She stopped herself from crying.

Feeney took the bucket of water and washed the cow's face. It gave itself up, dazed and exhausted. He cleaned off the hind legs. 'Go on now, you see she's fine.'

Maria waited in the yard amongst the pigs.

Feeney lifted the calf into his arms and took it out into the yard. The cow followed him. He had to stop and push the massive head back into the darkness. In the yard, the pigs were sleeping, the chickens with their heads tucked into their breasts. The sky overhead was black with clouds. He was glad. This was his secret.

Maria walked behind her father. 'You're not angry with the cow, Dad, are you?'

Feeney put the calf absurdly over the crossbar, its torso in the middle with the legs hanging either side. He extended the forefeet onto the handlebars so the legs wouldn't get caught in the spokes. It looked like the calf was steering. Feeney turned up towards the Gaelic pitches. Maria followed behind him. He stopped. 'You go home now, love.'

'Dad.'

'What?'

She turned toward home. 'Don't hurt the cow.'

Feeney swallowed and said nothing.

When Feeney finished disposing of the calf, he came back down to the yard. He locked the padlock again. His shirt was soaked with blood. His body trembled, blue with cold. The cow stood in the shed, waiting. In the yard, Feeney slapped the pigs and woke them. He threw stones to disturb the chickens. They flew around and then landed again. 'I want you to see what happens to animals who cheat Feeney.' The animals shuffled around, nosing the buckets for scraps. They were accustomed to order. The pigs tried to touch his hands. Feeney opened the shed and led the cow into the yard. He questioned the cow. He led pigs to an imaginary witness stand. He took hold of their hooves and shook them. The pigs grunted amiably, corroborating stories. Feeney got the lamp and brought it to the cow's face and then to the hind legs and told his version of how it all happened. Some terrible things had gone on in the yard. Feeney talked about the incontrovertible evidence, calling the cow 'a slut'. It stood with its head down in the middle of the yard. Its hind dribbled mucus. 'You have been sentenced to death.'

Feeney held the butchering knife in his hand. He took it to the neck of the cow and cut cleanly across the throat. The cow fell over like a cardboard figure. Its hooves tapped the concrete as thought it was impatient to die. Its mouth opened and closed mutely.

'Now there, justice has been served, Gentlemen of the Jury.' The pigs grunted around him. He let them smell his hand, the teeming sweat on the hair of his hand. He led the pigs into their pens, then left, locking the gate behind him, leaving the cow in the yard. He pushed his bicycle alongside him. He had done what had to be done. It was officially over. Now he looked forward. From the knackers he thought he would get enough for the new bicycle. He was adding figures in his head. There was always next year. The pigs were a sure bet. 'Gentlemen of the Jury,' he said in his most Protestant voice, then burst out laughing. The pigs had learned something from this. There was a contract in life, between all creatures, between men and women, between religions, between countries, between him and the town that had to be maintained, a life living on Borders. Himself and his pigs would continue through this time of struggle, in births and deaths, in the slaughtering and the eating. 'No,' Feeney said to himself. 'This wasn't a bad night at all.' It wasn't a thing to ruin a Christmas.

Ambrose Feeney had survived much of his childhood in the aftermath of the Second World War. His people had come to Limerick from their border town before he was born. They had endured the grim fatalism of the lean years, the blackouts and tea without milk or sugar, eating pig's feet and tripe. 'You could have bread and butter, or bread and jam, but not bread, butter and jam.' Life had its measured tedium.

The people had begun to ritualize hardship into religious fasts, sublimating the fact that the war was the creation of industry. They had turned from inexplicable war to inexplicable faith. But none of this affected Ambrose when he was content in his earlier years, before the illness, when he felt that life had meaning, that nobody was out to get him, that wars just happened and God loved him. It all came in a later stage of illness, after the denial of religion and before the hatred of mother. The sickness had a linearity which pleased him.

In those early years things had not been so bad. The humdrum boredom of life had its coziness. The fire drew the family close together, if only for warmth's sake. Ambrose liked that sullen comfort of want, the vague way people slowly rose up from lethargy to face the ineffectual nature of things that were either broken or about to break, the cracked milk jug, the warped back door that wouldn't shut and so let the rain run into the kitchen, the broken grandfather clock, his father's green bicycle with the slow punctures. That kind of impending frustration stood Ambrose well. Life dissipated into a dull parochialism. Ambrose's people had no car, so the world ended at the limits of what could be travelled in a day's walk or cycle. Even on the holidays, they didn't travel up to Dublin but further West to the edge of the wild Atlantic seaside resorts of Ballybunion and Lahinch.

Ambrose cursed the advances of technology, the cars, the radio and the newsreels for much of his troubles. It was hard enough to be exemplary within a city, to prove yourself better than any other person, without having to contend with far-reaching worlds where people did things under a different sun, lived in mountains or in deserts, spoke other languages – people more advanced, who wrote better, built better, or lived better than himself and his people. How could he take life seriously, growing up in his part of the world?

Ambrose spent his adolescent days as a brooding schoolboy in black trousers, grey socks and a heavy duffel coat, with no aptitude for school. St Peter's school was set far back into a field. Ambrose was impressed with the grounds, the pastoral setting, the long entrance flanked by grazing cows and sheep set between the goal posts of hurling fields. It was strategically placed, far enough away from women, where screams would only bother the animals, a dominion of men and boys.

The bleakness of the war had faded into the background by the time Ambrose understood what it was all about, its history consigned to the black and white of photographs and films, with only the occasional amputees around the city who had fought with England against the Nazis. There was a new generation of youth in the classes above him who had not been killed off. The memory of the war had reached a critical mass. There was enough of the present to taint its past. Of course, people didn't want their sons to die, but they didn't want them around the house forever either. Ambrose understood that the older lads were anxious about jobs. It was the first sense of helplessness he had encountered, the outside world impinging on the domesticity of his home life.

One day a politician came to the school and said, 'Lads, there are forces beyond Limerick at work in this crisis.' Apparently, there was some other town in Ireland making better sausages and bacon than Munster Meats. Ambrose was genuinely concerned with the state of affairs. His father was in their employment. Ambrose suggested a mascot, a pink pig smiling. God love him, Ambrose was ahead of his time, earnest in a practical way. The politician seemed on the verge of winking approval, his teeth showing. 'A mascot,' he said, beginning to move his head, but the priest objected and quoted the First Commandment. 'Thou shalt not have false gods before me.' Ambrose agreed with his vacant smile. The politician frowned. Ambrose slowly began to realize that modest lower-class living made everyone too religious; there was too much faith in rosaries and novenas.

Back home the same religion reigned indomitable, but with a more domesticated lunacy. The cult of Mary and St Philomena had set up shop there. The house, a shrine of Catholic ideology, had a wet glossy sign above the door that read 'Sancta Maria', for a house could be a woman. And if the metaphor needed an icon, it was there in the cracked statue of pale blue Mary, her thin foot on the head of a serpent, her hands outstretched, fed on a steady diet of adoration and petals. The supplicant St Philomena's head was curiously craned to the meter box on the wall. When Ambrose came home each day, there they were, ceremoniously displayed on the sideboard, the matriarchs of a patriarchal religion. As Ambrose was to say in later years, Feminism was invented by Catholics, when it was all said and done.

But Ambrose was oblivious to that sort of irony. All that came later. First and foremost, Ambrose loved the shambles of his house. It fell as a mollifying backdrop, camouflaging his grey and black clothes until he moved like a shadow. Anonymity was his companion. There were clothes strung all over the place, on chairs, on the banister, hangers on doors, clothes-horses with stiff socks and underwear, everything corralled near the fire, drying like dead hides. The indecency of it all appealed to Ambrose. Unreserved filth lived in open spectacle. 'Pure animal,' Ambrose said to himself.

From the kitchen the thick smell of the sweep-the-floor soup simmered on the blackened cooker, sundry items dropped into its warmth by his father who brought home scrapes of offal from the slaughter factory. The soup was now in its eighth year on simmer, an eternal cauldron topped up every day, the sediments of potato, carrots and meat turned with a wooden stick, always there to feed the hungry. Ambrose ate like an animal from this steaming pot. The sinews of his flesh had been made there, the skin on his bones to the hair on his head to the nails on the ends of his hands and toes. He marvelled at that fact alone. He estimated in later years that he was eighty-two per cent potato, eight per cent carrot, and the rest the unnamed meat of Munster Meats. The kitchen was set with rat traps, in the cupboards, behind the cooker and under the sink. As he ate, he sometimes heard the click of a trap in some dark place.

In these early years, Ambrose had set himself up with his mother. He hoarded his mother's affection, with dark stares at the remaining brothers and sisters. His mother was on to him as a good thing from the start. He knew that and was glad. He hated duplicity. She was a black hole of affection, a confectioner's dream, a lover of chocolates who picked her boy from the beginning. Ambrose had a sweet tooth to match hers. He said sometimes maybe it all began with the sweet tooth; it could have begun worse.

Ambrose loved the malaise of a family where the mother hated the father and vice versa. The black and white wedding picture on the wall said it all, his father tall and slender, his mother rigid in her own lace dress, two people facing forward, not touching, standing as two parallel lines that would never converge. That was how Ambrose came to see marriage. Ambrose had picked his side. It was always sons with mothers. There were a few on every street, boys who flanked their mothers everywhere. Some of them had grown into old men so that, when mother and son walked arm in arm around the town, you'd have a hard time figuring out if they were brother and sister or mother and son.

When the dances began to come around for the others, Ambrose stayed at home, his hands in the sink cleaning a pot or boiling a kettle or scalding a cup. He was a natural with domestic bliss, his time attenuated with all sorts of housework, sweeping the floor absentmindedly or rearranging the cups in the press, humming under his breath, using the floor brush to get at a cobweb wavering in the cold passage that led to the back door. The result was puttering. Life demanded the perception of progress and the sweat of true labour. The pure sensation of motion, the sweat gathering on the nape of his neck released the strain of what would have otherwise been a tortuous waiting game.

His father would be out the back of the house, perpetually in motion, moving blocks of wood from one bunker to another or feeding a few pigs. This restlessness had been passed on to Ambrose, no doubt, although Ambrose's actions had a more abstract quality. His mind romped while he worked. Much of the time he enjoyed himself. Another kettle of fish altogether was his father, a man afflicted with an almost ascetic nervousness, a pioneer and non-smoker, a man who slept on a flat board for his bad back, an animal slaughterer who sharpened his knives late into the night, knives which sliced animals' throats and buttered his bread. His father possessed that resolve of men born in poverty, when one instrument served all functions, and, as his father said, 'From laughter to slaughter there is only an S.'

As the nights settled, Ambrose wound down his activity with the splutter of the kettle. At the end of it all nothing got done. The kitchen was still a mess. Ambrose would stop to turn off the kitchen light, and he would go on with his Irish homework, the tea and bread, throwing a shovel of coal onto the fire.

Ambrose kept shy of his father, spending the night choking over guttural Irish words, looking earnestly at his mother who kept her head and her hands to the fire, with her hat and coat on her as though she was about to go out. Every so often, Ambrose's mother would correct him, making him twist his face into contortions and repeat some Irish word. Conscious of his limitations, that his burden was her burden, Ambrose demanded that she teach him what he had to know. His grievance was not known yet to either of them, although there was some unspoken tension living within close quarters, his mother hardly stirring, constant in her vigil by the fire, browning toast on a fork, supping hot tea which Ambrose brought to her in big, chipped mugs, a woman passing through the change of life, her coat wrapped around her body. Her life had spun down to one room, one chair, her presence inviolable. What emotions had passed through the placenta of an aging woman to a nervous fetus? What secret pact had they agreed?

'What's he at there, Ambrose?' his mother said, showing her horsey dentures, her clothes hot from the fire. Ambrose cautiously cupped his hands against the teacup. There was no sign of his father. Then he opened the kitchen door and saw his father sitting alone in his long coat at the table, his bicycle leaning indolently against the wall.

'He's sitting down, Mam,' Ambrose said softly. 'At the table.'

'Ask him if he's going out,' she whispered, feeling the cold air from the kitchen pouring through the open door.

'Are you going out, Dad?' Ambrose said.

His mother pressed his arm. 'Does he want anything to eat?'

'Do you want anything to eat, Dad?'

His father said nothing. Ambrose knew he wasn't asleep because he saw the fingers of his left hand moving. 'He has his bicycle clips on,' Ambrose whispered. His parents did not even speak to one another. Ambrose wondered what the hell it must have been like back then, when he first met her. How could things have changed so drastically? The very idea of the two of them, up in the room, his father grunting with his hat on, all business.

'We'd better stop awhile, Ambrose,' his mother whispered. 'He must be going soon.'

Ambrose's father let it all pass. He gave Ambrose a few good flakings for Ambrose's sanity and to ease his own nerves when these interrogations reached a point of absurdity. Sometimes he would be waiting for Ambrose to open the door, and grab at him by the scruff of the neck. Why his father took part in it all was beyond Ambrose. Ambrose's father tried to let matters see their own course. He knew that, for every few children born to a family, one had to be touched. There was always a runt.

Ambrose sat down with his book open on his lap and stared at his mother who stared at the fire. Behind them, his younger brother and older sister sat silent, studying without ever asking a question. Ambrose ignored them, only conscious of them in the intervals between going on about his own troubles at school and asking for his mother's help. He and his mother occupied the innermost sanctum of the roasting fire. At the outermost edge sat his brother and sister.

His father showed himself in the room. 'I'm off. There's coal enough for the night.' He set down a bucket of coal and stoked the fire. He went out when the kettle whistled and came back with a rubber hot-water bottle, holding it in his hand like a huge udder, giving it to his wife without a word. Ambrose's mother said nothing.

Ambrose's father squatted before the orange flames, putting his palms up against the fire for a few moments. Then he turned and stood up and warmed his back, breathing through his nostrils, his lips parting into what could have been a smile but turned cold. He scratched an itch on his neck.

Ambrose eyed him cautiously. His father scratched again. He had to warm his human skin before pushing his body out into the cold rain, like a dog warming itself before being banished to the outhouse for the night.

Ambrose swallowed and looked at the table, his legs trembling. If only just hating his father was enough. He used his hands to stop his legs.

His father's coat began to steam.

'Your coat,' Ambrose's mother croaked, only to get him to go.

Ambrose's father looked at her and then moved toward the door, tall and lean, his legs opening and closing with the stiff angularity of a compass.

Ambrose's mother rolled her sullen eyes in Ambrose's direction, her head immobile on her fat neck, her flesh hot in her coat.

The cold rain tapped the window outside. Ambrose listened to the bicycle being backed out the door. He saw his father in his hat and coat, diffracted in the tearing window.

Ambrose gave a sigh. There was no point feeling sorry for his father. He knew that, and yet he could not stop the shaking in his legs.

'Ambrose?' his mother whispered, breaking the stillness of the house, the ruddy rubber bag on her lap.

Ambrose had his eyes closed.

'Ambrose?' she said again.

Ambrose opened his eyes and looked at her blankly.

'Put on the kettle, Ambrose,' she whispered. 'We'll all have tea.'

It was during secondary school that Ambrose took on the name 'Tea Boy', a name he'd seen in a reader where an African boy served a fat white woman. She was always shouting, Tea Boy this and Tea Boy that. Somehow, in his tender years, Ambrose had been drawn to that name, a name that would become his epitaph. How sublime to be a servant to a good woman, to live in the claustrophobia of the house, to go out the back and get the coal, to dash up the road to the local for a bottle of milk and a few potatoes and a chicken leg for the stew. He'd have his newspapers in the morning and the evening and the wireless for a bit of entertainment. Jasus, wouldn't that be a great life?

At some indeterminate age, but early on, Ambrose had silently committed his mother to his own keeping, the way ducks take to whatever they see first as mother. He had no free will in it. He would move only within the city of his birth, always within twenty minutes' walk of his house. There was a biological territory beyond which man could not venture, the domain of animals marked by scent, his, by the length of getting to the shop to buy his mother some chocolates and back. The world could go to hell out there with its international disputes and its cold wars. He was sticking close to home. All he had to think up was a way to earn enough to live on.

School had to be coped with in the interim. There was little humour in school. Brother Bartholomew stood before them in priestly patience, an All-Ireland hurling player with an oiled wrist that could send a ball sailing or a belt cracking on flesh. The seminary recruited that kind of talent early in those days. Ambrose was petrified of Brother Bartholomew, or Brother Flick, as they called him. Brother Flick stood over him, toying with gravity, rocking from heel to toe. When he moved he gave off a billow of chalk dust. He stopped before boys and put all questions in terms of hurling, maths conjured as word problems: 'If you were going to buy yourself a hurling stick costing two pound and you invested two bob a week, with an accruing compound interest of seven and a half per cent bi-annually, how long would it take to buy the stick?' or 'How long would it take a ball, hit from a hurling stick, moving at forty-five feet per second into a headwind of twenty-two miles an hour at Croke Park during an All-Ireland final between Limerick and Kilkenny to reach the net, the ball being struck from the forty yard line?'

'Whose side struck the ball, Brother?' someone would always ask, scribbling frantically into his copy book.

'Limerick, boy. A Limerick shot on goal,' Brother Flick would shout, swinging his arms as though he'd hit the ball himself.

'First half or second half, Father?' Eyes roamed the class, watching the clock.

'Second half, Limerick down by two points with under a minute to go.' Brother Flick settled his hand on the crew-cut heads of boys whose scalps were checked weekly for lice, feeling the prickle of stiff hair, rapping his knuckle on the craniums of encased brains, breathing in the odour of medicated powder. 'Who's got an answer for me?'

It was during this time that Ambrose took an aversion to hurling and maths. He joined the ranks of stupidity down in Class C with its hardened thugs, thick farmer types, plain eejits and the misunderstood. There was no camaraderie among fools. Ignorance was unmasked to reveal the maggots of anger underneath. Pain isolated them more than it drew them together. The thugs smiled to hold back tears, smoked cigarettes afterwards in the toilets and went on about girls, while the rest settled down in despondency, waiting for the time to leave school and go to England.

School was managed. Ambrose did not protest violence, adapting into a somnambulance with his eyes open, since all that was asked of him was to sit up straight. Form was what the school wanted, an army of groomed Christians.

Ambrose persevered, having his few moments of humour, good laughs pulled out of nowhere. One day a priest was giving a talk on the evils of Communism, about the revolution in China under Mao Tse-tung. None of the boys was interested in China or Communism. It had been turned into a discussion on Paganism. The whole class couldn't pick out China on a map. Ambrose sat there, like simplicity personified, scratching himself out of boredom, the cold sunshine streaming in on him. The priest caught sight of him yawning. 'You there, Ambrose. What do you know about Red China?'

'Well, Father, my mother says it goes well with a white table-cloth.'

The class broke into hysterics. Even the priest didn't have the courage to tamper with that kind of genius. Ambrose had

31

his reputation secure with these one-liners, adding to the folklore of school. He was seen as a kind of passive dissenter, who might turn around at a later time and reveal something prophetic about his and other people's conditions. At least that was how Ambrose came to interpret his actions. He knew he had brains, believing that there was a machine inside his head which took care of life. For all the bad marks, he was not stupid. The school just wasn't what he found interesting.

Home continued in its elliptical manner, the fire burning on, his mother slowly cooking herself, inching ever closer to the flames, entranced. Stories about war atrocities were drifting over from Europe. It added to the gloom. As the politician had said, there were forces beyond Limerick at work. The principal industry was still slaughter, the city filled with animals being led from yard to yard, herds of frantic beasts, the roads dotted with fly-covered manure.

Despite everything, the priests fought to resurrect a sense of pride in the dirty-faced boys. They would go on about Limerick's great history, from the Danes, through the O'Briens, to Sarsfield's Last Stand, to the Flight of the Wild Geese.

Ambrose listened to the stories about Limerick women who had fought an enemy with pots and pans during the great siege of 1690. All around the city the remnants of the old walls stood, the vertebrae of a ghost city. Ambrose listened to it all, nodding his head, repeating great dates in Irish history, things that not even his parents had learned, dates that had been dredged out of library annals. Ambrose sat there letting the new history of his people enter his head.

One priest pointed out that the high incidence of haemophilia in Limerick correlated with the incidence in the different Royal families throughout Europe. Haemophilia was a disease of Royalty and inbreeders. There were only a handful of real Limerick names. He had cousins who were bleeders. It was not until later that Ambrose learned that mental illness also afflicted Royalty in great numbers, a limited gene pool, recessive traits, a breed apart. Psychologically speaking, there may have been some truth to the Limerick pedigree. The isolated intellect of himself and his people lay abandoned from Europe, a Limerick Galapagos.

At home Ambrose repeated the historical events he learned at school, his father, an ex-IRA man who had fought in the Civil War, being lectured by his son. 'What the hell are you talking about?' his father shouted.

'The conspiracy of the English. The famine, genocide. Brother Bartholomew says the Irish were the first to experience systematic genocide, not the Jews.' Ambrose sat at the table, moving his hands as he spoke, giving a feigned seriousness to his words.

'What the hell do you know about the famine?' His father was on his feet. The luxury of history was something he did not want to understand. Survival had occupied his life. 'What are they at, up there at that school of yours?'

'They're building the perfect Irishman,' Ambrose smiled. 'You have to know where you've been before you know where you're going.'

'Well, do you know where you're going?' Ambrose's father teetered, about to knock the head off him. He pointed at the ceiling. 'That's it for you. Those eejits up there are peddling ideas when they should be teaching you a skill, something you can live and eat by.'

'And what did hard work do for you?'

'You bastard,' Ambrose's father roared. 'Get out of my sight!'

Ambrose acquiesced and shut his mouth and went upstairs. His mother watched him out of the corners of her glossy eyes. Ambrose knew it was a game as well, accepting it as better than having to get his head kicked in for not knowing his maths and Irish at school. History provided those moments of reprieve, when all that was asked of him was to repeat dates and names with conviction.

History was still a schoolboy's game, with ballads sung,

> *Come out you Black and Tans,*
> *Come out and fight me like a man . . .*

> *A Nation once again*
> *And Ireland, long a province, be*
> *A Nation once again!*

Ambrose thought of all the useless hours in laced black boots pounding the upper floor of the isolated grey school as voices roared out the litany of Ireland's heritage, the secret names of Ireland, 'Dark Rosaleen, Cathleen Ní Houlihan.' And the jigs practised down in the gym hall, The Siege of Ennis, The Walls of Limerick, historical dancing and prancing, boys counting off, one, two. The ones pretended to be the girls, the twos the boys. 'Now step forward and back, and spin and move to the left and move to the right.' Boys pressed close together in sweaty intimacy, coiled greasy hair on dirty collars, with no rhythm in their stiff bodies, eyes slit, trying not to burst out laughing, kicking each other in the shins.

How did he let himself get caught up in such arseology?

Every Friday he was forced to move like a gobshite with his partner down in the hall and always under the threat of violence. He or his partner would get messed up in the dance, separate and move into the middle and stand perplexed, not knowing where to go, keeping their backs stiff, kicking their legs out in front of them, eyes looking frantically for a queue. Inevitably a priest would shout, 'And one and two, come on,' and take someone by the ear, making the boy keep dancing and yelping while being dragged into position. And all this for that one night when a girl would be substituted for a boy, the dance of procreation.

Ambrose was made to recite about Cuchulain and Leda and the swan. And the stories Ambrose could tell, mind you. But that was it for you, Irish nationalism, the most mediated birth of all.

For all of it, Ambrose was inspired by nothing. On his way home he still passed the old city walls sprouting tufts of grass, fallen stones nested in by birds, haunted by slinking cats, walls good for nothing except to duck behind for a quick piss, or to lean against to block the wind when lighting a cigarette. If there was one thing they did reinforce for him, it was that things were going to get worse before they got better. Limerick's former glory was over. He walked among its ruins.

At fifteen, Ambrose took a job at the local hotel, drifting out into the world of men. His mother watched him closely. They gave Ambrose a beautiful red uniform with brass buttons and shiny patent leather shoes. 'You look like an English admiral,' his mother cried when he came down and played the dandy, bowing and opening the door to his father who came bustling into the room with his bowl of soup.

'Look at your son,' his mother said, sitting beside the fire, her face glowing. Ambrose escorted his father to his chair. 'If I may, sir?' he said, pulling the chair out for his father.

'You may not, you eejit,' his father grumbled.

His brother and sister watched, stone-faced at the table.

Ambrose took on and off the white gloves he'd been given as part of the uniform and said, 'This whole thing has to be dry-cleaned.' Even Ambrose didn't know what the hell that meant. He went on with his game, the mimicry of subservience, the contrived ponderance of his every move.

Ambrose's mother smiled to herself. Exquisite manners and subservience were enviable in themselves. To be the best servant to a master had its own virtues. She had been the daughter of a cottier on an inland estate. Her book learning had taken her into Protestant households. Those early years had been a desperate attempt to put herself at the disposal of others, a coy Catholic timidity, an almost total submission to Protestant gentry.

Ambrose saw her teeth coming out of her head. He took her hand and put his lips to the rough skin. His father flinched.

He had money, he'd landed himself a job. It was a milestone. He hadn't wanted much at that stage of the game, just enough to keep going, to buy his mother the odd present, a quarter-pound of the yellow and pink powdery bonbons, to watch her drop them into her dark mouth, her dentures clicking.

Fitting in his schoolwork was hard, but manageable all the same. Although he occasionally brought luggage to the rooms for guests, he spent many of his hours at the hotel off in the toilets, cleaning toilet bowls and urinals – not that he told them that back at home. These were his first informed lies, the need to make himself more than he was. He said he was in charge of inspecting rooms to ensure that all the businessmen were thoroughly happy and accommodated. His father eyed him with suspicion but left him alone. The money was needed.

Now that Ambrose saw himself dressed up and saw the rich people coming and going from the hotel, he gave up the provincial ways of his former thinking. It happened in an instant, the freedom from the house, from the fire and his mother. Ambrose feasted on its characters. The hotel itself harboured possibilities, a strained cosmopolitan atmosphere of salesmen sipping whiskeys before visiting prospective clients, paunchy chaps in baggy trousers speaking about trout fishing, mingled with the yellowing decay of the afternoon tea set, old ladies sitting rigid by creamy lace curtains looking obstinately at one another and the bar with its laughter.

The hotel had the self-consciousness that Ambrose had always felt life warranted, all action under scrutiny, his obsequious presence on the periphery now, standing at attention beside a solid marble column, sociologist and busboy. The chandelier in the main hall held droplets of frozen light, giving a chill expectancy to whoever passed under it. They knew they were being watched. The chandelier divided the room into distinct quarters, a tangible effect created out of an intangible, there were invisible lines which were not crossed.

The waitresses bustled in their uniforms, attending to a variety of seated guests, moving with drinks on silver trays, followed by young men with platters of meat, slices of pink salmon, pale cuts of roast pork, fresh potato salads and decorative tomatoes stuffed with baby shrimp. Ambrose watched a gold trolley meander around the tables laden with fresh cut fruit and an assortment of sponge cakes, scones and flour-sprinkled currant bread. The potato in his own stomach turned hopelessly inside him as he waited to clear away half-eaten sandwiches, his torso extended over guests sitting cross-legged sipping coffee in small cups on dainty saucers.

By the time afternoon tea had been served, the chandelier took on a less radiant spectre, its light muted, casting a dull prismatic countenance on the place. It was then that the gold chain which hung across the entrance to an alcove off to the side of the main hall was removed, revealing mahogany tables with smouldering red candles. In this burrow night entered its own domain, the women in long evening dresses, hair styled, smelling of perfume, and their male consorts. They were all foreigners with some loose connection to Limerick, many there to sell off an old estate or auction off family heirlooms.

By dinner somebody was always shaking drunk, sputtering nonsense, and had to be helped to bed.

Ambrose spent all his weekends down at the hotel, witnessing the transformations from breakfast, to lunch, to dinner and beyond. Aside from the guests and the hangers-on, Ambrose was enthralled by the salesmen who came to stay, arriving with heavy suitcases full of all sorts of commercial products and gadgetry. Either the worst or the best at what they did, Ambrose could never decide. He would lead them up to their rooms, pointing out the attractions, the picture house and the boat that went up the Shannon if they were intent on some fishing. They usually tipped well.

Ambrose took the money, aware that it was not theirs, not that it mattered, but the way in which they handled it bemused him. He took the money without looking at it, his hand feeling the delicate weight of the coins, calculating the sum in his head.

By the time the salesmen finally came down, they were stripped of human oil, skin pink, tips of the fingers withered, perfumed with what eventually passed for bad liquor. Ambrose or some attendant showed them to tables that should have been occupied by at least another person, although each salesman ate steadfastly alone. There were maybe fifteen or sixteen of them set off to the side during the dinner in their own dominion every night while the other tables were crowded with loud and shrieking women and men toasting this and that. Jesus, it was a far cry for Ambrose from the 'lick-the-plate-clean' candour of his own people.

If he was allowed to stay over one of the nights at the hotel when things were busy, Ambrose could linger in the hallway, stealing glances at the guests. After dinner the dining room ensemble smoked at the bar, the young women and their dates, and the salesmen swirling scotch and water with an uneasy hand, sidling business into pleasure, trying to present cards. The salesmen nodded congenially toward one another, hair obediently combed to the side, some with small toothbrush mustaches twitching between a smirk and disdain, all amiable adversaries, until their necks were sore and their arms were limp from shaking hands. If there were 'no bites', as the salesmen put it, then slowly one or two and then a few more would ask Ambrose where the docks were, and off they went stiffly, full of Limerick's best food and drink, down to where the prostitutes lingered.

Had they any education at all? Ambrose put the question to himself a hundred thousand times, mimicking the very tone and stylized posture of the salesmen in the bathroom mirrors. Whatever his marks at school, here was a way out into the world of hotels and grand slap-up meals. This seemed to be the future of business: creating need. There had always been want, but need was something far more concrete. The product was there before the consumer. Ambrose felt he had charm enough to lug around the invention of some company and present the need for it to women. Hadn't he anticipated his mother's longings all these years? Yes, he could do that. Success in business demanded a congeniality. It demanded men of character and taste, subdued and polished, men demonstrating a machine that a woman would use. Oh yes, it took a rarefied creature to pull off the subtlety of femininity in the mask of masculinity, but Ambrose knew he was up to the challenge.

In the interim, Ambrose continued to drag slop back from the hotel bins outside for his father's pigs.

41

A swooning sexual inadequacy slowly manifested itself as the weeks passed. Somehow money, or the idea of money, was always tied to sexuality. Ambrose had developed a need to be near these young women, with thin ankles and luscious red lips which they pencilled on in the bathrooms he ended up cleaning when the hotel closed for the night. He found the paper tissues with the imprints of kisses and put them to his own lips. He lingered in the offing, listening to their giggling and whispered conceits, watching their intolerable tenderness hanging on to the arms of men. Ambrose was always there with head held high when a drink was requested. In this realm, money was never exchanged. The gentlemen gave a room number, speaking without looking at Ambrose, the observant phantom. Everything was delivered on silver trays, sparkling glasses filled with champagne or wine. There was never any physical contact, a strangeness which began to afflict Ambrose. Maybe he really was in a dream. It was 'skin hunger', the need for all human interaction to begin or end with an animal pawing or sniffing, a handshake, a continental kiss.

Ambrose slowly found himself brushing against women as time went on, in the lifts and hallways, lewdly apologetic, a diviner drawn to water. These women possessed their own gravitational sphere, delicate creatures who when they walked could crack marble with the force per area of their dainty mass localized on the nibs of stiletto heels. Ambrose moved within their orbit, smiling. Maybe one of these women would take an interest in him, a cheap romantic dream of being seduced by a rich beauty. He had no cologne as such, but when he happened to get into a room he dabbed himself with some salesman's cologne or, if need be, sprayed himself shamelessly with furniture polish, an agreeable lemony odour. He also wore fresh underwear throughout the entire period in question, just in case.

Why couldn't he do something with himself? He spent hours looking in the mirror. Why? The first sense of inferiority passed in its blackness as he sat in the women's toilet, crying to himself behind a stall door. He had gone there to stave off the anxiety of having been shouted at by a young man in front of three women. They had laughed at him and called him 'Country Thick' for spilling a drink on a young woman's evening dress. Even he could see now that the uniform was the kind of thing grind organ monkeys would wear, a cheap generic uniform with loose threads, the trousers with the legacy of different hem lengths marked from all those who had worn the uniform. He'd really been led down the garden path with this one. Ambrose felt the ironic joke of his uniform, a crude approximation of some anachronistic time of English generals and admirals, the fake gold embroidery of the sleeves, his lily-white hands sticking out to open doors, mimicking the very nation that his country had fought so adamantly to rid itself of, and here he was, Limerick shithead prancing around the place. What psychological satisfaction, what libertine justice to have history and pomp at the service of new wealth!

43

Two women came into the toilet, and suddenly Ambrose realized that he was trapped into the bargain. He hadn't put up the sign outside the toilet saying it was being cleaned. He couldn't very well come out now from a closed stall with not even a bucket or a cloth in his hands. He crouched on the toilet seat like a bird perched in a cage.

'Are you going with him tonight?' one woman giggled. Ambrose listened to the click of the high-heeled shoes on the marble floor.

'Are you joking? He doesn't have a penny to his name. It's all his father's money.' The woman went into the stall beside Ambrose, and he stiffened. He heard the scrape of her silk stockings being pulled down. He saw the curve of her arched foot in the high heel in the next stall. His own legs burned as he squatted over the toilet bowl, listening to the chill champagne of earlier in the evening squirt into the bowl. It had its own alcoholic aroma. He bit his lips, thinking of the sprinkling cascade, the pressure of her delicate stomach, the pucker of her navel. There was no stopping him at this stage. What if the other woman went for the stall? He felt he should say something in some squeaky voice, or make a slight cough. But wouldn't the woman look down and see no legs?

'That Frank Mitchell is studying to be an architect,' the woman giggled, her words echoing in the toilet.

Ambrose knew she was drunk.

'Oh, an architect! Have you seen his erections?' The woman outside the stall burst out laughing.

'Stop, will you before they hear us. Don't you think Frank should take me out?' The woman pulled at the toilet paper, blotting the urine droplets. Ambrose felt his groin churning, inches away from the woman. His knuckles were white, his fist

44

clenched, his mouth half-open, taking in the aroma of fear and urine. He heard her pulling up the stockings. She flushed the toilet and left.

Ambrose's legs buckled on the bowl. He went out of the stall, shaking, and took a rubbish bin, pretending he was cleaning, whistling to alert anybody who might come through the door. His lips were parched. He reached the door on marshmallow legs and went straight out the back of the hotel into the cold night air. The ambivalence of laughter or crying passed through him. He swallowed his Adam's apple, safe at least. Wind swirled around him. The stupidity of the whole thing, to have walked in there in the first place . . . Jesus, where was his self-control, insatiable eejit? Imagine what the police would have done to him? He'd have ended up a cripple. The coolness of the night brought a slow awareness back to his body. Never again, he resolved, tapping his foot against the concrete.

And still his head was filled with the notion of the girl. He had not seen her, but he would always remember the beauty of her sounds, her voice, how she would not give herself up without a price, the sheer condescending lilt in her voice. It was this emotional ventriloquism which captivated him. It seemed a woman's prerogative, chameleon femininity, the mask of makeup and perfume, creatures who could transform them- selves, a suggestive charm that did not define itself as much as it asked to be defined, asking whatever touched it to leave its mark on it. And this wasn't just there with women. If Ambrose had hidden among rich men, he was sure he would have heard the same words, the same elusive grandeur of deception.

A lesson had been passed down to him in that absurd place. As he perched on a toilet, a world had opened up to him where he saw that things defined themselves by what they were not, not by what they were. In that instant, all his thinking had been undermined. He felt like crying.

He'd seen this deception all around him for months, the Englishmen in weathered canvas jackets, worn tweed trousers and old hats, slaphappy old boys going off on fishing excursions or hunts like collective vagabonds with canvas bags for tea and sandwiches only to come back to dress up in dark black suits for six course meals in marble dining rooms, nails manicured and skin glowing. They loved to flirt with two identities. The absurdity of compromise was beyond them. Wealth, like religion, was ethereal, outside of nature, something that could not be wholly grasped or understood. Its ubiquity was its grace, its elusiveness its exclusiveness. Ambrose shook in the mute acknowledgment of these things that passed before him and knew there was something severely wrong with himself. He would have left there and then, but what could he say to his father? If he stayed, it would only be to get the slop for the pigs.

A servant girl came out into the back and began to smoke beside Ambrose. He could feel her looking at him in the darkness. 'Are you all right?'

Ambrose had his hands buried deep in his pockets. 'Yeah.' He felt his eyes moving under the lids.

'Could you walk me home tonight, Ambrose?' she said. She was a thin girl with an undefined oval face, something that looked half complete.

Ambrose swallowed, looked at her, shivered and said nothing. The moon drifted off in the distance. He could smell the river, the algae exposed at low tide down at the docks.

'Do you want a cigarette?'

Ambrose shook his head standing in the cold bleakness among the rotting odour of the spoiled food.

The girl breathed smoke through her nostrils. 'So are you going to walk me home?'

Ambrose turned and looked at her, an ugly girl from the Island Field smiling at him. He'd been a step away from getting himself jailed back in there. He'd been saved, not through some volition of his own, but through pure chance. Would he have struck one of the women, or both of them? He gnawed on his lower lip. Jesus Christ, was his sanity contingent on chance? He had the potential to do anything.

'Will you walk me home?' the girl said again, curling her damp hair behind one ear.

'I have to get my homework done,' was all Ambrose could manage finally.

The girl drew in another breath of smoke. 'They're talking about you inside. The way you look at the posh. Mr Neill says you make them feel uncomfortable, like you hate them.' She let a smile set on her face, relaxing, her thin torso set on bony hips.

Ambrose wanted to go back inside again to get away from her, but she put her cold fingers on his sleeve. 'Walk me home, won't you?'

His arm stiffened with her touch.

'I won't say anything about inside.' The girl looked pathetically at Ambrose, as if embarrassed at her own blackmail. 'Just walk me home, will you?'

Ambrose could see she was serious. Ash sifted through the darkness, falling on the white tongue of her pinafore. A gold button on Ambrose's coat popped off.

The girl dropped her cigarette and turned to go inside.

Ambrose touched her arm. 'I'll walk you home,' he

whispered. 'I just have something on my mind.' He showed his teeth in a forced smile.

'Your lip is bleeding,' the girl whispered and went inside. Ambrose stood still, the sham military-uniformed hotel piss boy standing with the conviction of a captain at the helm going down with his ship. He swallowed the sweet blood, running his tongue over his bitten flesh. He tried to turn his head and found his body paralysed.

Later that night Ambrose asked the girl to meet him out back. He took a flower from a vase in the dining room and hid it under his coat. He didn't want her to say anything about him. He stepped out the back and gathered the old potato peels and put them into the two metal buckets he always took up and hid out the back of the hotel. The girl loitered, smoking another cigarette while Ambrose searched for any bits of bread in another bin.

'I have to take this with me,' Ambrose said, turning to her. 'Do you mind?' He took the flower out from his coat. He had crushed it, but he gave it to her all the same.

They walked quietly down by Barrington's hospital and off toward the Island Field, his fingers gripping the cold metal handles of the buckets.

'Why doesn't your father come up and get the stuff himself?'

'He's busy,' Ambrose answered curtly. His shoulders were aching.

The night cleared up as they left the city. Even the stars were visible.

'Do you ever wish upon stars?' the girl said, slowing the pace.

Ambrose swallowed, hardly able to endure the walk and her

49

carry-on. The stink of the old potatoes added to the discomfort. They passed a pub filled with laughter and shouting. 'I'll leave you here then, all right?'

'A little further,' the girl whispered.

Ambrose finally stopped near St John's castle, put down the two metal buckets like a man disposing himself of his conscience, put his tongue into the girl's mouth and leaned her up against the old wall, almost lifting her off the ground. She was on tiptoes. His dirty hands held her thin wrists, her body writhing underneath, their teeth grating. Ambrose caught the glint of the moonlight in her wide-open-eyes. Ambrose smiled to himself, she hadn't even the mind to close her eyes and think of someone else. The two buckets stood like mute sentries beside him. Maybe she really wanted him, feeling that he was no better than her. Ambrose worked the hot spittle of his kiss with hers until she was on the point of suffocation. Her head was pressed against the wall. Then he withdrew his tongue and pulled back his mouth. She gasped for breath, her lips glossy with the juice of his kiss. His cut had opened again. Her pinafore had a thread of his blood on it. She rubbed her wrists which had been marked with his handprints, but it didn't stop her from smiling eventually and asking him in for a cup of tea and to meet her parents and her six brothers. She said it was the least he could do for her.

Ambrose took up his buckets of scrap and went and had tea in her kitchen and met her brothers who asked him what his intentions were, winking at him.

Ambrose said his intentions were honorable. It was the only thing he could come up with, something he'd seen in a film down at the Savoy.

'I want to become an architect,' Ambrose announced the following day, recovering from what he later called his first bout of metaphysical distress.

'I want to become an architect,' Ambrose said again. The disconsolate image of his mother roasting by the fire made him wild with hatred of her and of himself for ever having loved her, a deflated sack of meat, farting on her sagging seat, digesting the breakfast, dinner and tea of fifty-odd years, a bladder of sugared tea in her. Christ, he'd set his sights short. It was the first time he felt he could have killed her. If there had been nobody in the house, he'd have hit her with the poker and told her what an ol' whore she was, what a banjaxed ol' fuckin whore she was to have conceived him and brought him into this hole of a place.

His mother looked up with a hat crowned with fresh roses from her garden firmly planted on her head, an army of statues around her. 'What happened, son?' She passed a glance in Ambrose's direction.

'He met a girl,' his father said. 'What's her name?' His father put a potato to his mouth, his eyes squinting.

Ambrose burned with embarrassment, his sister and brother sitting on the couch, looking silently at him.

'You've lost him now,' his father said in an unmodulated tone, bringing a huge mug of tea to his lips.

'I want to be an architect,' Ambrose said again, feeling his chest heave under his shirt, sweating at his own inadequacy and at the thought of them laughing at him.

'You mean a bricklayer,' his father smirked.

'No!' Ambrose shouted.

His mother's face soured.

Ambrose saw it. What he would have said if he'd have had the nerve . . . He felt his head spinning. Sufferin' Jasus, a poker on the back of the head weren't good enough for the likes of them, a gruesome twosome, sick fornicating animals, spawning the likes of him to roam the planet. Did they ever think about what they were creating up there in that room? Oh, by Jasus, he saw it all, his father in his boots, anchored to the floor, the lubricant from his bicycle chain on his dirty stained hands, and those dentures dislodged in anticipation of ecstasy, a grinning skull. As if seven children weren't enough, as if he didn't hate her enough already. 'I want . . . ' Ambrose could not get the words out.

His mother brooded, staring into the fire, alarmed as Ambrose grated his teeth. 'Who put that notion into your head?' she said, turning again to Ambrose. The fire danced on her shinbones.

'Nobody!' Ambrose's voice quivered. 'Why can't I be an architect?' His face was numb.

Ambrose's father pointed his knife in his direction. 'You couldn't draw tea.'

Ambrose turned to his mother. 'Why can't I be an architect?' he said again.

Ambrose's father was still pointing the knife. 'Watch it, do you hear me? It's that hotel up there. You've been there morning, noon, and night. You just sit yourself down now and give yourself a dose of life.'

'You have to be sponsored to be an architect. Do you know that?' his mother said, shuffling her body in her chair. 'And the parish priest would have to sign something, and . . . who's going to sponsor you, Ambrose? Where are you going to get the money for it?'

'I can do a correspondence course,' Ambrose shouted.

'What are you talking about? You're not even finished school!' his mother croaked, putting her hands together.

A loose rain began to fall like someone spitting in fat splats against the glass.

Ambrose's father turned in his chair, his face gaunt. He put his knife down on the plate and then tensed his fist, turning the glob of potato and grease in his mouth, his eyes blinking. Ambrose could sense his movements even as he stared at his mother. His father got up and swung at him, the fist grazing his chin.

'Stop it!' Ambrose's mother roared, knocking her tea off the arm of the chair. 'Now look at what you've made me do!' she wailed.

Ambrose's father stood like a sprung trap, looking at his wife, his hands hanging loose off his shoulders. 'Get out of my sight,' he shouted.

Ambrose whimpered and then slammed the door and ran upstairs. The night passed with roaring downstairs, what passed for a monologue, his father's voice saying this and that, although Ambrose knew his mother was nodding her head or making some gesture by the abridged silences between his father's words. Ambrose moved his jaw back and forth with

53

the palms of his hands. Then his mother began wailing out prayers, and an almighty fight broke out. 'Let them fight.' It was better than the obstinate silence that reigned otherwise. Doors slammed. Then the gas meter clicked, and the house went dark, and silence fell. Ambrose listened to his father climbing up onto the chair in the hall, feeding two crowns into the meter.

Ambrose waited for things to settle, until he heard his father down in the kitchen with his knives, sharpening them against a dull stone. Ambrose went to the bathroom and turned the taps and filled the basin with water and washed his hair and scrubbed out his ears. He was filled with emptiness. The filth of the house brought on a greater despair. Maybe he was trapped. Three of his brothers had escaped to Australia and a sister was in Canada. Ambrose's eyes burned with tears. He scrubbed his face and neck until they hurt, shivering in the cold darkness, the squat toilet before him. The condensation on the window shattered the moonlight into fragments. His father was only feet away from him downstairs, separated from him by the floorboards. He could hear the sound of the knives and the pigs outside.

Ambrose tensed his body. The rich had a refined posture, a way of walking with their heads in the air. He shivered in the coldness, his body set in goose pimples, the blue veins near the surface of the skin. The melancholy image of his mother downstairs remained. He was the son of a pig slaughterer, the son of a dirty old peddler of religion, a woman who washed with holy water. Even he could not see himself as an architect. He saw himself as a victim of bad genes. That was his favourite place for laying blame these days. Ambrose moved in the darkness, stripped like some religious pilgrim, his damp clothes in a pool on the floor, and perched on the yawning porcelain bowl, trying to bring back that image of the girl. The entire bowl shook. The moon jelled on the glass.

'What the hell are you at?' his father roared, prodding the ceiling with the floor brush.

Ambrose's eyes filled with tears, the absurdity of himself squatting over the place where his family planted their arses and shit out the digestion of their days, feeling his own long coiling intestines connecting into the pipes running down the back of the house and into the secret underground life of the city sewers.

When Ambrose came out of the toilet, his father sprung again, a blow across the face that drew blood, a slaughterer's accuracy. 'No son of mine . . . '

Ambrose – Limerick's first existentialist man, as he would come to call himself in later years – whined, then stiffened and crept off in his underwear, his clothes under his arm, the blood dotting the cold floor, a boyhood menstruation. He had come of age as he curled up in bed beside his silent brother.

The following day, the door was off the hinges in the bathroom. Ambrose dressed and left without eating and ran up to the old walls to relieve himself. Then he continued to the hotel and handed in his uniform. They charged him five shillings for the fake gold button he lost.

On the way out, Ambrose passed through the breakfast room and looked at a salesman, seated with his Hoover, nodding his head as though he were agreeing with something the Hoover had observed.

As the weeks passed, Ambrose's mother even got up on occasion and made Ambrose a cup of tea or went down herself to the local to get him a bit of sweet cake when they had the money. She wasn't going to lose this son. She tried to get what was wrong out of him. Ambrose was fanatic at his studies, the first hint of anger seen in his shaking legs. It couldn't have been a girl. It had to be something more, a fit of youth, or Limerick madness?

'Will you stop shaking the table?' his father shouted. He was getting scared that he had trouble on his hands with Ambrose.

Ambrose just stared at his father blankly, his eyes glazed, always about to say something, his head pounding with the unfathomable exercises, the fatigue of mental stress. His mother looked from the fireside and put her weak lips together and wet them with her tongue. It seemed she was in constant prayer, but Ambrose knew she wanted sweets. She wanted her old Ambrose back. Ambrose saw the lips but was afraid to go and get her something since his father was watching him. His mother tried her best to keep Ambrose content, to get him to the point where he could start supporting her. And for all of it, Ambrose could not bring himself to truly hate her.

At nine o'clock Ambrose's father announced he was going out, that a shipment of animals was coming in on the train. His father went into the kitchen and set the water on to boil so he could shave. He wouldn't be back until the next morning. For some reason his father was adverse to letting hair grow on his face.

'We'll have tea with what he doesn't use,' his mother whispered.

Ambrose got up to release the pressure on his legs and the anger in his body. He was his father's son, no doubt about it. He paced back and forth in the hallway looking at his father leaning over the sink shaving himself and then rubbing his neck, then passing his hands over one another the way Pontius Pilate must have washed himself of Jesus Christ. His father washed only his head and hands, exposed flesh. Ambrose knew there were parts of his father's body which had not seen a sponge in years.

Ambrose went back into the sitting room and stood near the fire. 'He's still shaving,' he said.

His father appeared again, his jaw red. He limped slightly as he went to the clothes-horse and took off a shirt. He'd developed pains in his legs from the nights out on the bicycle and had taken to carrying a cane. He used it not as much for walking but as a crude feeler, letting it scan and prod things about him, the way the wheel of his bicycle ate up the road in front of him. Extensions of himself were always arriving before his body. He prodded Ambrose between the shoulder blades. 'Make sure you set the fire for the morning, do you hear me?'

Ambrose winced. 'Right.'

'There's sawdust out back on the sheet. Make a pile of coke snakes and pack them tight.'

Ambrose watched his father spraying his shirt with a mist of water and then holding it close to the fire to take the stiffness out of it.

His mother closed her eyes and feigned sleep.

'What are you looking at?' Ambrose's father said to him, turning his head mechanically back to his shirt wavering before the heat.

'Nothing.'

Then his father put the hot shirt on his body and almost grinned with satisfaction, slipping into his coat, trapping the envelope of heat between the layers. 'I'm off.'

The evening set into a soft blackness. 'You'll have tea?' Ambrose's mother whispered when her husband left. Her head was working to bring some solace back to her own life. She had to reclaim him for herself. All she had were her prayers as a form of persuasion, pushing her hopes through forced miracles. She could say nothing of her own will. It had to be said according to the will of God. That was the recognized difference between men and animals. Men used instruments to their own ends. She was further along, with her statues and her abstract religion.

Ambrose's mother went out to the kitchen and put on the

kettle. The cauldron of soup bubbled away on the back ring. She had two shirts and a pair of socks simmering in another pot which she took out with a pair of tongs and put under the cold water and wrung out.

Ambrose saw her out in the backyard in the cold air, the clothes steaming. She hung everything up on the line. He wanted to go out and tell her he was sorry, that he had his sweets upstairs and that he'd forget about being an architect. The fire burned softly before him, easing his head. Ambrose stood up and took a deep breath, nodding imperceptibly to himself. He had to give up his grievances against his parents. They had done only what others around them had done. His father had provided a house and food and clothes for his family. They were none the worse for all that had gone on in their midst, the proper domesticity of meals on time, a good fire and cups of tea and bread. So what if they couldn't stand the sight of each other? They accepted that without condition and proceeded from there. His mother and father were under no delusion that things could have been different. This was the best they could achieve. His father had his work, and his mother, her religion.

His mother worked slowly outside, the sky heavy with clouds.

Ambrose followed her out the back and opened the shed door where the pigs came to life, sniffing his hands. He went into one side of the shed away from the pigs and sat down on his haunches before two piles, one of sawdust and the other of coal dust. He scooped both heaps into a metal bucket. There was old newspaper which he tore up and added, turning it with a stick. Then he added a little paraffin to dampen the mixture. When it was ready, he stood up and took a hollow pipe and jammed it into the bucket, forcing the mixture up the pipe.

Ambrose's mother came and stood behind him. 'I'll get things started. Do you want a bit of soup?' She smelt of laundry soap when she put her cold hand on his neck.

'Yes,' Ambrose whispered, his back to his mother, hitting the hollow pipe against the ground, the long wet snake of fuel coming out onto the ground.

His mother went inside, listening to the tapping of the pipe, vaguely content. She stirred the soup, scraping the remnants of mashed carrots and flecks of meat from the bottom of the cauldron. Then she emptied the pot which she had used for the clothes and refilled it and took another pile of clothes, yellow shirts and underwear, and put them into the pot. She peeled away at a block of white soap over the hot water.

Ambrose came back in with a sheet of newspaper spread out in his hands. He had made nine snakes of coke. He went into the sitting room and set them far enough away from the fire that they wouldn't ignite but would harden. He passed his mother in the kitchen scooping out a bowl of soup for him. A moment of serenity passed between them, the peace of working in harmony. He passed his hands under the freezing water, and began to cry without a sound.

His mother saw him and said, 'Did you get something in your eye?'

Ambrose twitched his nose and squinted his eyes. 'I did.'

'Go on in and I'll bring this in for you.'

Ambrose's mother set down the plate beside Ambrose at the table. It was one of the few times he saw her standing up for an extended period of time. She moved slowly, as though she were remembering how to walk.

Ambrose ate the soup, shaking.

'Do you want a bit more?' She had another bowl in her hand.

Ambrose took the bowl and pinched some salt over it.

'And there's a bit of bread here, son.' The table trembled as she cut into the crust, shaving off thin slices which Ambrose accepted and dipped into his soup, dredging for flaking bits of carrot and meat.

'And you'll have tea?'

Ambrose knew she was going to say something to him. He stared at the teapot in its woollen cozy.

His brother and sister looked up from their books, always present and mute.

'I want all of you to do one thing in this world,' his mother whispered. She took the pot of tea and poured Ambrose a cup.

'The strainer. You forgot the strainer,' Ambrose said flatly.

His mother put the pot down and took a spoon and caught three floating leaves. Their eyes met for an instant.

Ambrose tried to get up. His mother smiled and put her hand on his shoulder. 'We're out of sugar for the rest of the week. Do you want a bit of honey wax?'

'Just milk.' Ambrose swallowed. His mother never attended to him like this. Ambrose had his finger through the ear of the cup. She poured the milk, and it ran down the side of the cup, over his fingers, and pooled in the saucer.

Ambrose removed his fingers from the ear of the cup and rubbed them against his trousers.

'Remember that God has a plan for all of us. We cannot demand things which have not been ordained.'

Ambrose had his head down, penitent. The soup settled in his intestines.

'Are you going to drink the tea or look at it?'

Ambrose brought the tea to his lips and drank.

61

'The man who goes against the will of God is damned for eternity.'

Ambrose knew the words were for him alone. He stared at the crescent of dirt still under his nails. She was telling him in her own way that he was never going to be an architect.

'There are jobs in the Civil Service for you. I have prayed for years,' she whispered. 'Good jobs if you work hard at school.' She put her hands on Ambrose's back, like some sort of faith healer, a saint who interceded on behalf of humanity.

Outside a dog barked.

The cup trembled against the saucer. He took it to his lips and emptied it without tasting anything. His mother had a flower in her hand, something she had found out in the back garden. He smelt its fragrance, the bruised petals where her fingers had squeezed the juices. She passed it before his eyes. She read flower petals like gypsies read tea leaves. Each petal held a secret petition which only she knew. She revealed only the truly apparent, the sure bets. Ambrose looked at his brother and sister out of the corner of his eye, always there in what he called prominent obscurity, the two who needed nothing from their mother. Ambrose knew he was a beaten man. They would escape, but he never would. He had given himself to her, and she had silently responded. 'Since you have nothing else, son, take me.'

'Jobs are there for you. You're fortunate. Be thankful to God for that.' She made no bones about it, that she was committing herself to her children, that the debt was owed her. All these years had been in anticipation of being taken care of when the time came. She trusted eternity to God and a living to the Civil Service.

'I want you to make a promise to me that you will do God's

will,' she whispered. She held the flower in one hand and poured an arc of steaming tea into Ambrose's empty cup.

Ambrose nodded his head. 'Right, Mam. You know best, Mam.'

'And what's best for you, Ambrose?'

'A good steady job, Mam.'

'And what else?'

'To pray for faith, Mam,' Ambrose answered, as part of his rote catechism.

'And among your own people,' she said flatly. 'What would you want to be an architect for?'

'I wouldn't, Mam.' Ambrose said, breathing through his nostrils, the tea and flowery aroma wetting his eyes.

'You didn't know what you were thinking, Ambrose, did you?'

'That's right, Mam, I didn't know what I was thinking.'

'So what do you want, Ambrose?'

'A good steady job among my own people, Mam.'

'Right, Ambrose. And you're going to pray to God for that?'

'Right, Mam. I'm going to pray to God for that.' Ambrose looked up plaintively, entranced by her look, her face devoid of irony.

'I think you should go to bed now,' she said into his ear. The new cup of tea sat untouched.

'What about setting the fire for the morning?' Ambrose said.

'I'll take care of that, Ambrose.'

'I think I'll go to bed then,' Ambrose said, rising up from the table.

'And we'll all be praying, won't we Ambrose?'

'We will, Mam. We'll all be praying, Mam.'

'Praying for what, Ambrose?'

'Praying for a job with the Civil Service, Mam.' Ambrose left the room and climbed the creaking stairs, tipping his head to avoid the hanging light halfway up. There was nothing like the Civil Service. He nodded his head. Even its name suggested an accommodating, friendly environment, a fraternity of easy-going, sedentary, long-lunching, holiday-taking characters. He took a deep breath as he undressed. Give her money for a few years, then he'd get himself a woman in time and bow out as an honest son. To think of it, a wife to cook his meals and give him children, good holidays here and there, and maybe a car down the road. It seemed so elemental as Ambrose pulled the blanket over his shoulders, curling up, hugging a pillow, an imaginary wife.

From the shops up the town, he could get goods on the hire-purchase, paying pennies over a lifetime for things he needed, installment payment schemes. The salesmen had distributed their goods, enticing customers into lifelong com-mitments to things like toasters, lawnmowers, and washing machines. It would all come to pass in the next few years.

From the darkness of his room, Ambrose tried to pretend he was dead, pulling the blankets over his head, stretching out on his back. But from downstairs came the scrape of dishes, a basin of water being splashed against the wall outside, the sombre grunt of the pigs in the pen near the coal bunker wanting bits of food. The soft hiss of a bicycle tyre passing by on the rainy road outside filtered up. They were eternal Limerick sounds, nothing new or different from other years, sounds his parents had known as children. It was hard to believe that two world wars had passed his country by, that somewhere out there people were making atomic bombs for another war. If he pressed his eyes with his fingers, he could see the static and then sudden bursts of light amid the darkness of his faked death.

The struggle in school persuaded Ambrose that he was a limited man. Maybe his mother was right after all. He fled once more to the sanctuary of home. Despite himself, the habitual ritual of the chocolates began again, first in a shy embarrassment. Ambrose put sweets into his mother's purse, leaving them stuffed down beside her chair, sending her cards in the post with pressed petals. His mother let it happen in its own way, smiling, acknowledging his homecoming, the symbiosis of her Catholic world coming together perfectly with this son. She pressed her wishes on him softly, talking to him about landing soft jobs that would keep him close to home and God, repeating the bleakness of what her life had been, how she had been forced to move from town to town during the war. And God-lover that she was, she had a right to it, no doubt. She'd outlive her husband, just like most of the other women. Ambrose looked at her blankly. She was speaking as though his father was dead. And then Ambrose had a queer fancy that maybe there should be some amendment in the way age was calculated for men and women. Dog years were seven to a human, but how about a man to a woman? 'Yes, Dan is now forty-five, that's about sixty-three in women's years.' You see, you could not blame her for her ways, the dread of years of loneliness, of being discarded up at the town home for unwanted people.

'Are you listening to me, Ambrose?'

Ambrose looked attentive for a moment, listening to her say the same things over and over again. It was how women got their way.

His mother fought many unseen battles amidst her family through all those years. From her chair by the fire she had slowly tried everything she felt she was good at – drawing, writing, acting – with a secret belief that she had some hidden talent. Her pockets were filled with scraps of paper, odd rhymes and little poems, all this silently conceived and tried by her in the squalor of her sitting room, the cups of tea and greasy plates all around her, the clothes drying by the fire, herself lost in her own world. What Ambrose had unconsciously felt all his life, the doubling experience, she had made into a principle for life, consciously making herself leave her body and enter into the engine of her head, dabbling here and there. Yet, since she never announced she was thinking anything, her sedentary nature seemed imprisoning to those who did not understand her, so that with each failure only she obliquely noted it and then went on to something else in her endless pursuit of her destiny, never despairing because her one sure bet at the end of it all was her progeny, the debt of children.

Ambrose came to realize how vicious competition had become among everyone looking for jobs. There were long hours of grinding homework. The school offered a study hall at night to ensure that everyone was working hard. Ambrose went to it from September through Christmas, labouring over his work. This was the last year to sort things out. They were the sixth year. Bullying prevailed to release the tension. The first- and second-year students had to run messages for the older fellows. A system had slowly evolved where the hard-core cases were now set in their ways, making money from all sorts of things up at the school. This was their testing ground, where they established their reputations. There were fights at the handball alleys out the back of the school, fights set up by the gurriers. Who was claiming who? Bets went around all day long throughout the classes. Ambrose participated to the extent that he had to, shouting and jeering with the rest of them. The fights were all hushed up from the priests as the classes waited in anticipation of a good one.

The absurdity of the matches didn't matter. Two softies drew as much of a crowd as two goers. The softies were even more fun sometimes. Two big fellows would go down and take hold of two softies, grabbing their hands and making them slap the face of one another. That really got the crowd going. They spat down into the pit, 'Come on, you Nancy Boys!' Then their heads would be smashed together, and it started in a frenzy of girlish hair-pulling and shrieking, kicking and then headlocks and fists.

At other times it would happen spontaneously. Ambrose would be in playing handball with a few others, and along would come a pack, dragging or pushing two fellows in front of them. 'Everyone out, do you hear me?'

Someone had fouled someone in a game of football or some stupid thing, and that was all it took. Ambrose or anybody else had to come out of the arena, and then one of the thugs would announce the fight from up on the walls. The throng surrounded the pit, as they called it, and bets were spat upon over handshakes like horse deals. Someone watched for a priest. 'Get it started, you eejits. He'll be back in a few minutes.' Ambrose tried not to watch, shouting his head off in an obligatory fashion, spitting into the concrete coliseum. There were no easy falls, and each time the stronger fellow hopped the head of the other against the walls, blood ran out of the nose. There was never any surrender, fights lasted until someone gave the word that a priest was coming. The bleeding fellow would be abandoned in the alley, left cowering and weeping only to be found by the priests who would demand answers to questions which no loser could ever give, and then the second beating began, the echoes of priests' shouting and the boy's pleading.

Of course, nobody could play handball until a good clean rain came and washed away the blood. Ambrose would be left bouncing his ball outside the alley looking up at the sky, saying over and over again, 'Does it look like rain to you, Tommy?'

bouncing or squeezing the ball to harden his palm for the game.

'It does, Ambrose, it does. We'll play after school surely.'

'If there's not another fight.'

'You never know, Ambrose. You never know.'

And then Ambrose's mind would fall back on the maths problem he'd been doing in study hall for the few hours, and the tension started again.

School ended in a modest Leaving Certificate, nothing great, but Ambrose had proven himself better than half of his class. The commitment of those arduous nights of study had paid off. If there was one thing that could be said for Ambrose, it was his earnest heart. Ambrose was in the kitchen, drinking tea and eating beans, when the postman came to the door.

'It's here,' his sister shouted, taking the letter. His father was out the back, feeding a rubber tube through a basin of water, looking for the tell-tale bubbles where the puncture was. He stood up in his black suit and V-neck jumper and came to the back door. 'Dad, Ambrose has his results.'

Ambrose opened the envelope and looked at the marks and then looked up without expression.

'Well?' his father said.

Ambrose held the paper out for his father. His father looked at the marks and showed his teeth. 'So we'll have an architect yet.' He took Ambrose's hand and held it firmly, the hand cold from the water, the thin fingers and hard knuckles moving under the skin. Ambrose's own hand was warm from the cup of tea. His father's eyes, a sad blue, smiled, showing a former youth. His father still looked handsome, something Ambrose only realized at that moment. But he averted his eyes like he had done down at the hotel and looked at his sister who peered from the doorway.

'You've set yourself up well, now. There's an envelope up in my room in the top drawer. Get it for yourself,' his father said softly. 'But don't let on anything to herself.' His father took his hand back and went out to the inverted bicycle and began working on the puncture again.

Ambrose went upstairs and found the envelope tucked under the wax paper in the drawer where his father kept his socks. He took the twenty pound note, a huge damp bill that smelt of feet. His father must have kept it in his boot when he went on long trips up the country. Ambrose puffed up his cheeks. His father was hard, there was no arguing that, but . . . He stood in the dim light of the room, holding his breath, feeling his heart thumping in his chest, the dull sunlight netted in the curtains. His father's life had gone wrong, not by something his father had done, but by circumstance, the great wars. He remembered the story his sister had told him of the severity of risks, of doing one thing over another, of the Christmas when his father slaughtered a cow and went mad and nearly got run out of town up the North. That was before Ambrose was born, but he always imagined his sister out in the barn with his father, thinking of the strange things his father must have done to raise his family.

Ambrose was glad now that it was all over. His father had tried to settle things. He had the decency to end the years of frustration with a handshake. It made things simple. Ambrose pulled back the curtains and saw his mother out on the street in her hat, her arms sloped from the weight of two bags of food. She had begun to move around in the warmth of the approaching summer months as she did every year. He could hear her high-pitched voice. With her was his younger brother, Desmond, a fat boy in Ambrose's hand-me-downs. Ambrose let the curtain fall again and went back down to the kitchen and poured another cup of tea, feeling freedom trembling inside him. His sister watched him and said, 'So, you're going?'

Ambrose drank his tea. He would have the money soon enough for his own place, to set himself up with a bank and get himself a house if he wanted. He wouldn't ever be up at the big hotel, except for the occasional meal or town dance, the odd wedding reception, but he'd have security, the thing his mother had yearned for all these years, the thing that had evaded his father. He would never want again. With one sheet of paper, his life was guaranteed. It seemed ludicrous, but not something he could scoff. The shadow of middle-age descended on him. His father was out the back with his bicycle, fooling with rubber tubes, trying to ease his nerves, lost in a perpetual chain of things about to break or broken, everything sublimated into an obsession with odd jobs. Ambrose listened to the hiss of the pump, the door rattling on its hinges. It was a situation which could bring happiness or madness, depending on the circumstances of Ambrose's head, and he knew it. If he had been a drinking man, he would have gone out and gotten drunk, but neither he nor his father were that way.

When his mother came in and read the results, she bawled her head off. There were fellows with half his marks who got good jobs. Ambrose was a sure bet now. She took him into the front room with all the portraits of the family, the wedding and communions and confirmations. 'Thank St Philomena for what she did for you,' his mother said, taking his hand and making him touch the slender, polished girl toes which his mother kissed when things got so bad that she felt a miracle was not coming her way.

'Yes, Mam,' Ambrose said in his contrite way, her hands pressing his. He wanted to say, 'It's because I studied until two in the morning for nine months straight that I got my marks,' but instead just tipped his head and gave thanks to a dead Italian girl for a modest Irish Leaving Certificate.

'I want you to make an offering,' his mother said, looking at Ambrose.

Slowly, Ambrose took the warm bill out of his trousers.

'An offering to St Philomena for what she did for you,' his mother smiled, her hand closing over the note.

'Yes, Mam,' Ambrose answered. Then she left and went off into the streets with the results, waving them in her hand. Ambrose's father came back in through the kitchen, wheeling his bicycle. 'I'm going uptown on a job,' he said, tipping his head. Ambrose stepped aside and watched his father pass. His father was just going off to cycle himself into exhaustion out on old country roads, driving the pistons of his legs all night, the flutter of his dynamo on the back wheel registering the electrical current of his nerves, a solitary light, a great Limerick luminary, moving in a disconsolate orbit around Limerick. If he and his father had been normal, they could at least have gone fishing like some of the others on the street. But his father had taken on a life of animal stoicism. Ambrose watched him going, the curve of his back hunched over the handlebars.

Ambrose sat the Civil Service exam a fortnight later in Dublin, and by the end of the summer he was accepted into the Civil Service, a job in the Department of Agriculture and Fisheries. Ambrose had mentioned university, half-heartedly, he had to admit. But there was to be none of that. His mother bawled that she had raised him, had sacrificed for him, and how could he do this to his mother and father? 'It's a sin.' He received a uniform measurement form from the government in the post and that had sealed everything.

Ambrose entered the realm of the employed up in Dublin, out in a remote area, in yet another uniform, a smart fisheries officer's jacket, the gold leaf stripes on the sleeves, the creased trousers and spit-shined boots, the same anachronistic attire of a defunct past. He was going forth, not to do something for himself, as much as to reconcile the prayers and petitions of his mother's religion. His work was a manifestation of divine intervention, the years of prayer answered in the flesh and blood of a provider. This is what the Civil Service stood for, a windfall of secular miracles coordinated by the government to ensure the sanity and stability of a nation. Poverty could not be allowed to afflict successive generations without apocalyptic consequences, a hatred of religion and violence. Ambrose began to understand that procreation in human society was not so much about preserving the species as it was about making sure that there was someone to take care of the old. All of this weighed down on Ambrose, a man in the grips of an inarticulate atheism, a man living in the shadow of a mushroom cloud, in a world flirting with Armageddon, a man who loved and hated his mother. He visited the neighbours, taking away words of wisdom and good luck. Ambrose bought one more large box of Black Magic. He wasn't beyond the effects of irony. He promised his mother he would send home money.

His mother came to the station in a pale blue dress, like some squat Madonna. Her face had lost all youth, the candour of her eyes earnestly on her miracle, her son. Ambrose stood at attention in his uniform, commissioned with his mother's faith. He turned, and his father took his hand. His father wore his IRA veteran medals on his black suit, the resolute hero of poverty past and hopelessness. Ambrose stopped himself on the verge of tears. The platform was full of sons leaving their parents. The station master blew a sudden shrill whistle, and it was as though a whistle had sounded for a race to start. Ambrose turned and left his people.

Is the mind a time bomb? Can events drive a man insane, or must there always be the propensity for madness? In other words, was madness there all along, waiting for a particular environment to bring it to the fore? Young men are always leaving their mothers, it is a part of life. And Ambrose had a good Leaving Cert and a steady job. What he lacked was a woman, but is every bachelor a lunatic? It might have been the lighthouse at the end of the pier, the regularity of the flash, incessant, day and night. But Ambrose never really had to see that. He lived down below in a small round room with two other men who were none the worse for it.

Ambrose was sending money home on a regular basis which, again, is not a sign of madness. Others were doing the same as himself. The isolation of the commission was for only two years, and then Ambrose was guaranteed a new position, so it wasn't the anxiety of having to live in such conditions for the rest of his life. In fact, the money was so good that he could afford to put money into a savings account, on top of the money he was sending home. He had a soft life at the end of the pier, even he had to admit it. All expenses were covered.

The depression set in that first winter. Ambrose woke up early every third morning, rotating his shift with the two other men. The darkness of the morning did not lift until past nine o'clock.

Ambrose set his alarm for half-five and woke up into a dark quiet that was even more still than his dreams. He turned on a lamp beside his bed. An oily yellow light washed over the room, the sea lashing up against the solitary porthole window. Sometimes he lost his balance in the room, wading across the cold stone floor as if he was seasick. It had all the auguries of solitary confinement, something to which no man wants to awake. Ambrose dressed in his uniform without washing, shivering as he buttoned the cold cotton shirt around his neck, feeling the itch of stubble on his chin, fixing the knot of his tie in a small mirror by his bed. His socks were often damp, so he had begun to sleep in them and only changed them occasionally. Since dry shaves had begun to give him bad rashes, he shaved the night before so he still looked presentable for the morning.

From the window he looked out to sea, the grim porthole always tearing, the warped illusion of the monotonous miles of sea and the clouds drifting unseen overhead in the early morning's milky luminescence. He put his face up against the cold glass. A lone light from a ship passed somewhere out on the sea. It seemed ludicrous to have to get up, but there were boats and fishermen getting ready to venture out before the night lifted. Raw and unnerved, Ambrose's stomach turned inside him. It was not even eight months since he had finished his exams, but already that life had receded into the past. The feeling passed through him most days, but he thought that it was nothing to do with being homesick, that it was a feeling shared by all men who woke to the monstrous sea, that it was something he would get used to as the time went on. Spring and the summer would provide a different window on the world, the porthole glimpsing a clear blue sea.

Ambrose hated the morning shift, having to creep around with the soft swish of the light above scanning the sea incessantly. He moved under that great Cyclops. He stepped out of his room into circular living quarters. A big wooden table that looked as though it were hewn from driftwood was marooned in the centre of the room. A small cooker and a sink were set by a window. Ambrose went over to the cooker, took the kettle and filled it from a tap connected to a barrel of rainwater outside.

The rainwater was tainted with salt. The tea was never any good. Ambrose sugared the life out of it, trying to get rid of the salty taste. By the small porthole window he sat eating a bit of brown bread, looking over the choppy sea at the men in overalls lugging boxes and nets onto their boats. With every few minutes, the scene cleared. He began to identify faces. The fishermen had a system worked out where one of the boats would sound a whistle when they wanted the customs official and fisheries officer to come over. Ambrose listened to the wheeze of the short-wave radio. He went over to the round barometer, checked the pressure and noted it in a ledger. He would have to pass on the information to the fishermen.

The whistle sounded. Ambrose buttoned up his coat and stepped out into the grey salt air, the wind tugging at him, almost toppling him over. He had never learned to swim. He had picked swimming as one of his hobbies on his Civil Service exam, but had never dreamt that his answer might have got him his posting. He had nightmares about slipping on seaweed, or of a huge wave crashing up on the pier, sweeping him into the sea. On his next holidays he was going to take lessons.

Ambrose marched down the pier, self-conscious, feeling he was a ridiculous spectacle, dealing in law and mandates with hardened, leather-faced fishermen who reeked of the sea and fish guts. This was a place beyond laws. What would they say behind his back? Still, Ambrose persisted. The more insecure he felt, the stiffer his posture, the firmer his footstep as he marched with his head up down the pier and around to the side where the trawlers docked. The mornings were usually rainy and cold. Ambrose was often soaked through by the time he came around to the men, his face reddened, his eyes watering. His ceremonious job was to check the nets in different boats, to see that they were regulation size, while the customs officer on duty made sure that no alcohol was being smuggled along the coast. Sometimes Ambrose was helped on board, a fisherman taking him by the elbow and shoulder, securing him as he stepped onto the rocking boats and checked for lobster pots or illegal poisons often used to drug schools of fish, as the customs officer looked for guns for the North. What if he had seen something out there, in the early morning darkness? What then? They would probably have drowned him and the customs officer.

That was about the extent of the job. When a catch was unloaded, Ambrose and the customs officer followed an inspector from the Department of Health who picked up different fish, putting them to his nose as though his nostrils were an official instrument. Ambrose kept his arms hanging down by his side, the hands in loose fists, looking stolidly, moving his eyes between the different vessels. He was genuinely embarrassed at the spectacle of himself and the other two government officials rummaging around in a boat that could barely hold all three of them. The inspector was openly taking bribes in Ambrose's company. Ambrose had to look away and pretend he saw nothing, although he knew that the inspector wanted him to see how the place was run. The customs officer often went up with the inspector of Health to the local pub where the inspector had some other scheme going. Ambrose knew he was set if he could just keep himself in with the other two officials, if he could just keep himself from undermining everything that had come to him in the past eight months. The fishermen were hard workers who seemed to respect the officials and their uniforms. They took pride in being inspected or at least made a good show of it, as if it raised their status, to think that the government cared enough to send so many departmental figures to keep Ireland's fishing industry running. The conversation was always directed to the weather, though. Everybody knew the extent of the job, and, as long as that complicity was preserved, life could proceed as usual. Ambrose could continue to come out on his useless morning patrols, greeting the men and watching their vessels waddle out into the ocean. The fishermen always gave Ambrose some shrimp or cod for his troubles, and Ambrose took it home and cooked it with potatoes and peas or beans. Ambrose fought against himself. Jesus, there were men who had been turned down for this commission, men who had failed the Civil Service examination and had nothing.

A good-looking face did a lot for Ambrose. It relegated any morose aspect of character into a formal dignity which the fishermen regarded as part of a good education. They often hinted that they had girls at home who would come down and show him how to cook. Ambrose obliged with smiles and winks. He said when he got settled he'd come up by the pubs, as there was lots to be done out on the lighthouse.

The fishermen left Ambrose standing at attention, fighting the shaking in his body and thinking it was the coldness of the salt air, looking up at the painted houses, the bleached pastel colours of fishermen's houses, children hanging around kicking footballs, girls with prams playing mothers. Ambrose was trying to take in everything, trying to understand the fishing town, to situate himself on a pier on the edge of a coast and say that he belonged there among them, a place he had never heard of before, a people he had never known, trying to convince himself that all this was meaningful, that he was being paid good money to make sure that these people obeyed the international laws.

Something snapped inside Ambrose's head. The burning cynicism of his earlier years left him. The longing for love and attention abated without crisis, without even a roar, just a constant humming sound, and a slight downwardness of the head as though he were looking for something. He went off on long walks. The sea was so vast that it hurt his eyes. The land never had that effect on him. There were places upon which to fix the mind, to stare and wonder – who lives there, or what is this or that? Time decompressed, each movement in his body registering as he walked along the coast road. He was conscious of his body first, the pressure of his feet inside his boots, a stone pressing on the sole. He stopped and hopped around, unlacing a boot, trying to find the stone that was aggravating him so much, and found only grains of sand. Then it was his veins, the slight throb behind his knees, under his armpits, his pulse at his plump neck, or itches that made him stop and rub himself like a dog with fleas. He had songs from the radio in his head which disassembled in his mind until he was left with just useless notes.

The dementia of his youth, the taking apart of things like train sets and clocks to see how they worked was now turned onto his own body, inward into his head. But the joke in all this was that he was getting paid for these walks into insanity. Life had come a long way in one short generation. Ambrose felt almost immoral, taking money for a job like this when he looked back on what a generation before him had lived through. But why contend with this guilt? Why force himself to answer for what had been done to people like his father and mother? Ambrose was caught up in severe disbelief of everything around him. His will had no part in anything. Circumstance dictated everything. If he could have said, 'Yes, you see I did things differently from my father,' he would have been content. He would have seen some progress, but there was no plan. Then a sudden shower would drive him into an old shed somewhere for half an hour or so, and the cold rains would drive everything from his head.

Of course, Ambrose knew he should have been looking to the future, not lingering with something he could not comprehend. Everything would progress, with or without him. Ambrose blamed religion, as other great men before him, for the sense of time and history that had been forced down him, the burden of history predicated on an event, the Crucifixion of Jesus Christ and even further back to the notion of Original Sin, his history, a cross-reference of accusation and hereditary guilt. If he could have, he would have had his head turned about on his body, looking back at where he had come from. When he got on these kicks, he knew there was something wrong with himself, the propensity to turn actual life into abstract meaning, to disassemble a religion to serve his own end. What the hell was he playing at? Did he believe even a quarter of what he was on about?

Of course, interesting things went on from time to time. Ambrose wrote home about the trip out into the bay on the trawlers to rescue a herd of cows which had stranded itself on a sand bank when the tide came in. He had never known that cows could swim. However, he talked about the loneliness most of all in his letters home, inarticulate attempts at explaining how he felt. His mother wrote back to him that he should say his prayers. That would occupy him. Or he should think of her back home with his father. She never asked him directly for money. It was always under the guise of lighting candles for him or having a mass said in his honour.

It was good to have the two other men, Brennan and Doherty, at the lighthouse. They took turns cooking, washing the dishes and cleaning. They had a domestic pride in the lighthouse. Their chatter kept Ambrose in the realm of the sane, despite his long walks. He had to be back for meals.

A few of the girls from the town began to come down to them on a regular basis. There was a crate of vodka Doherty had got from a trawler a month back, which, of course, had been put there by the fishermen to bribe Doherty. He kept the vodka in the crate but had it hidden. When the women came down, he went out and brought in a bottle.

One night, before the women came down, Brennan said to Ambrose, 'You'd better give up that lark sending money home.'

Ambrose ignored the remark, sitting at the table, reading the newspaper. The hum from the light above filled the silence.

Brennan was a slim, ugly fellow with bony shoulders. His uniform did not fit him well. The seat of the trousers pulled tight around his backside, forming a visible V-shaped wedge at his crotch. Brennan was saving his money to enroll himself in university. He shared Ambrose's disdain for the job. His commission was one long study hall. At first, Brennan thought that Ambrose was onto the same game. He tried to team up with him so they could get the better of Doherty, but Ambrose didn't want to implicate himself in anything. He grew cautious of Brennan. He didn't want to lose his job, no matter what he thought to himself. Money was money.

Brennan wrote in his accounting book, cursing from time to time, trying to carry numbers in his head, tapping his pencil on the table. He was doing a correspondence course. Ambrose continued to ignore Brennan, reading the news from home.

Then Brennan looked up again at Ambrose and said, as though he had been formulating the sentence for ages, 'I know it's not my place to say it, but you should be looking at that Catherine Mallory. You won't do better than her.' Ambrose pretended to be engrossed in the newspaper. Brennan got up and stretched himself, casting a shadow on the paper. Unseen above them, a wheel turned the great light round and round. It set the cadence of life for those down below. Ambrose followed the swish of light unconsciously, staring at the paper without reading. It took two seconds for each rotation.

'Well, what do you think?'

Ambrose ran his tongue over his teeth. 'Don't worry about me.'

'It's not worry, it's friendly advice, Ambrose.'

'Well, I don't need it,' Ambrose said without moving his head. Outside the sea had begun to pound the coast. When the air teemed with a taste of salt Ambrose knew they were in for a night of howling wind and rain. There would be no chance to get out of the lighthouse for a walk. Already his legs were beginning to shake.

Brennan broke the lead of his pencil on his copybook and cursed. 'Stop rustling the paper, will you? There's absolutely nothing in the papers that concerns us.' Brennan slowly turned the pencil in a parer. His face was beet-red with frustration. He had no way of ever asking for help on any of his problems. A wrong answer or a dilemma took sometimes three weeks to get resolved. He'd have to write off explaining where he was stuck, hope the weather was all right for a boat to cross over to England, hope that his question was interpreted correctly, and then wait for someone at the university in England to write back to him. Ambrose often saw Brennan sitting around the lighthouse talking to himself, trying to drag some complicated answer out of his head.

Doherty came into the tower, head bent, rubbing his hands together. 'We're in for it tonight, fellas,' he muttered.

Ambrose looked over at Doherty as he shook his oilcloth coat and hung it up on a stand. 'I saw the girls down below. They'll be up in a bit if the weather holds,' Doherty said, looking over at the two men sitting silently at the table, the door rattling behind him.

'It's bad, is it?' Ambrose asked distractedly, rustling his paper to annoy Brennan.

86

'The waves are crashing over the walls. I hope it lets up a bit so the women can come out.'

Ambrose moved his paper into the light again and tried to read.

Doherty was a rotund figure with a blue tinge to him like a creature lacking oxygen, his face pinched into two thin lips which came to a small O, a sinkhole in the centre of his face. What the other men lacked, he made up for in a friendly, frank demeanour. The kind of man who deserved this position, he kept the place lively.

Brennan looked at the paper. 'The *Limerick Leader*! Jesus Christ, would you look at this, Doherty? I'd swear he's homesick.' Brennan let out a feigned sigh of despair, trying to get in with Doherty.

Ambrose went on reading silently.

'Are you two at it again?' Doherty shook his head. 'Jasus, if two men can't make an effort to get along together out in a lighthouse, what hope is there for the rest of humanity?' Doherty came forward, his weight sinking to his middle, his legs bandy, balancing his topheaviness as he walked. He went and put a hand on Ambrose's shoulder. 'He's a better man than either you or me. He has consideration for others.' Doherty staggered where he stood, his face red and sweating. The smell of drink filtered through the salty odour of the room. Doherty was out to get himself a woman, not a gorgeous woman, just a plain woman with a need for respectability. It was part of the equation of the Civil Service.

Ambrose felt the pressure of Doherty's hand. Doherty wanted them all to be friends.

'Listen, I'm putting you straight about money, Ambrose. A girl expects her man to have something to his name,' Brennan continued, sitting down again at the table with his books opened before him. 'I'm just trying to help you.'

'Give over,' Doherty shouted, looking at Brennan. 'To each his own. What's your interest in our Ambrose here anyway? And where's your woman?' Doherty slurred.

'I told you I have a woman back home waiting for me,' Brennan answered, burying his head in his books again.

'A queer woman who doesn't write you a letter now and again,' Doherty scoffed.

'Maybe she's illiterate,' Ambrose smiled, allying himself with Doherty.

Brennan glared at Ambrose, but Ambrose knew Brennan's game. He'd seen this sort of thing back at the hotel, the desire of a certain breed of man from a poor family, from a bad part of the city, to educate himself and move on and start over again without a thought or a care of where he had come from. What Brennan didn't need was to be reminded of his origins. To have the likes of Ambrose around undermined everything he was trying to do. Ambrose had the same sort of problem with Brennan. Ambrose had his perceptual pasts and Brennan had only conceptual futures. Doherty was left with the present all to himself.

Ambrose pretended to read the paper, the battle lines drawn. Doherty had staked his claim on the lighthouse. He wanted to stay there, drinking with the fishermen, taking money for allowing the fishing nets to be woven tighter to get more catch. There was no way of turning Doherty in, since Civil Servants were notorious for getting themselves into a place and then using their influence for their own end. Ambrose knew that he and Brennan were the problem, not the job as such. It was grand for those who could take it.

'They'll be up soon, and look at this place, for God's sake! Come on, the two of you, pick the place up. I don't want any more of this, do you hear me?' Doherty pointed his finger at Brennan, staggering slightly.

The night brought in a howling storm, the wind lashing the porthole windows. The lighthouse seemed to sway, the wooden beams creaking. The three of them were silent, icy stares passing between themselves and the walls. They were all dressed in their uniforms, riding out the storm.

Ambrose put his hands in his pockets and went to look out at the sea, from the porthole in his room. He could see nothing in the darkness.

Brennan took out an accounting book and began reading. Doherty brooded, rapping his fingers on the table, stirring impatiently on his chair. 'Will it break, do you think, Ambrose?' Doherty shouted.

Ambrose appeared again at his bedroom door. 'I don't know.'

Brennan had his head bent, mumbling to himself.

'Close that book, do you hear me?' Doherty roared. 'You're in the employment of the Civil Service, commissioned for idleness until further notice.' Doherty broke off laughing.

Brennan shut the book, the blank candour of his stare unflinching. He was dealing with a question two weeks old. He didn't need the book to go on thinking about it.

'You'll wreck your eyes. There's not enough light,' Doherty said, easing his voice. 'Turn on the lights, Ambrose.'

The lights flickered and then sustained their glow.

'I don't think the women will get up at this rate. What do you think, Ambrose?' Doherty looked resigned to the useless night. He got up and turned off two of the lights, making the room fall into shadows. A solitary bulb glowed near the cooker.

Brennan stood up, his slant shadow impressing the emaciation of his body across the floor. He took his books to his room and returned to his seat without a word.

'I don't think the women will get up at this rate. What do you think, Ambrose?' Doherty said again.

'It doesn't look good for them now,' Ambrose whispered, coming down and sitting at the table, breathing slowly through his nostrils. If only he could have told a joke, but he could think of nothing to say. Ambrose felt genuinely sorry for Doherty. If it had been just the two of them, Ambrose felt he could have said something funny or at least gotten Doherty started, but Brennan was there to make him feel self-conscious, to knock the whole thing off-kilter. Yes, Brennan was the problem. His presence disturbed the equilibrium of the place. Doherty's good nature could not counter Brennan's presence as well as the gloom of the sea and the non-prospect of the women coming up. Ambrose stared at Brennan, that worthless creature. If something happened among them now, if a fight broke out and he murdered Brennan, he could fling the body into the sea, and nobody would ever think foul play. Ambrose mulled over the image of Brennan studying. Except for Doherty's presence, morality could be suspended with the storm. And with the way things went, Doherty was often passed out by midnight on these terrible nights, drunk out of his head. Anything could happen out here. If Ambrose wanted, he could damage Brennan. It was one of the few times in Ambrose's life that he felt in control.

True to form, Doherty brought out a bottle of vodka from his room and put it on the table. 'Will you have a drop?'

'I don't want a drink,' Brennan said obstinately. 'We're on duty.'

'Go on, will you,' said Doherty. 'You old dog-in-the-manger.' Doherty began to pour out some vodka.

'I don't want it straight. Make mine weak,' Brennan protested, getting up for water.

'I'll make mine stronger,' Doherty grinned, topping his glass to the brim. Then Doherty settled in and began drinking and telling stories about his family. He had come from a large family of girls who were always sending him puddings, recipes for fish pie, and jumpers in the post. He shared everything. As long as he had his drink, he moved in its current, drifting and bobbing along until he thought of something to say, giving the illusion of movement, a true stream of consciousness.

The night dragged. Doherty and Brennan were well into the drink when Doherty looked over at Ambrose and said, 'What the hell's with this pioneer lark, Ambrose? Jesus Christ himself was a drinking man. Come on and have a sip, will you?' Doherty leaned back in his chair, his glass balanced on his stomach. Brennan sat upright, tipping his head, nursing his own drink.

'It's been a tradition in our family,' Ambrose said softly. The thought of killing Brennan had passed. 'There's a history of alcoholism in our family. It's got nothing to do with religion at all, really.'

Doherty's head lolled on his body, his small lips opening to receive the vodka. He poured the drink into himself and then brought his eyes to meet Ambrose. 'Come on, Ambrose, we can't relive the sins of our forefathers. Wasn't that what we learned from the war, too many people with too many obligations? The only thing you should take from your people is their name.'

A wave lashed the outside walls, and a plate fell off the sideboard. 'Jesus Christ,' Doherty muttered. 'What weather. What weather. One day we'll wake up with our beds in the sea.' Some leaks had already appeared in the plaster, dark mildew growths where the sea had split the stone.

Brennan smiled a wry smile of inebriated contentment. He hadn't heard the plate smash. He looked at Doherty, 'We're on our own in this world, amn't I right?' He smiled and rolled the whites of his eyes. 'I'm going to show them back home what . . . what I'm made of . . . You . . . mark my words . . . We're on our own . . . '

'Some more mercenary than others, no doubt,' Doherty answered, winking at Ambrose. Brennan's head jerked on the thin stalk of his neck. 'What's your problem, Brennan? You were no good at hurling and took up schoolwork instead, is that it?'

Brennan shook his head. 'Give me a few more years, and I'll put you in your place, Doherty. I'll . . . '

'Maybe you've had enough.' Doherty smiled. 'He's some bastard all right. Keep shy of him, Ambrose. He's dangerous, and God knows he may actually get somewhere in this world despite his temperament. I've seen worse do better.' Doherty took the drink from Brennan and put it before Ambrose. 'Come on, Ambrose, there's only the three, no, the two of us, yourself and me. He'll remember nothing in the morning. Have a drop.'

'I don't want to become an alcoholic just to please you,' Ambrose said, standing up.

'Neither do I, Ambrose. I want you to become an alcoholic to please yourself.' Doherty licked his lips, the tingling sensation of the night and the sea outside adding to his own state. 'You're a sad case, Ambrose. Get whatever it is off your chest with a drink in you. It'll do you a world of good.'

Brennan's eyelids were already dropping. He took the bottle from the table and tried to put it to his lips. The vodka ran down his chin. He had drunk only to ally himself with Doherty.

'Jesus,' Doherty shouted.

Ambrose reached out and took the bottle out of Brennan's hand. The hand fell limp on the desk, as though disembodied.

Doherty loosened his belt and breathed hard. 'Am I to be the last one left standing?'

If there hadn't been a storm, Ambrose would have run out of the lighthouse.

'Ambrose, old son, appropriate misery, and God knows there's enough of it, to some small period of time where you can let it say what it wants to say. Get drunk and sit back and let it all out. The time of martyrs is past. Brennan's a gobshite, but you, Ambrose, you could have it all if you would just let yourself live for the day. There's women down there that would fall over their knickers to get a man like you. It's not love you're holding out for, is it?'

Ambrose rolled his eyes. 'Do you take me for an incurable romantic?'

'Well, you'd better get on it now.' Doherty resettled his sagging trousers on the roll of his stomach.

Ambrose tried to smile. 'Yeah, you're right.' It seemed ludicrous to be taking advice from the likes of Doherty.

Doherty grinned. 'I know I'm right. Jesus, time is passing us by, Ambrose. That Condom train that went up to Belfast last week is the beginning of the end for the likes of you and me.

Imagine if women could choose their man. We'd be banjaxed! Amn't I only telling the truth? Look at the head on me! We'd be reduced to a shower of homosexuals.'

Ambrose felt obliged to wink back.

'Listen, Ambrose, this is it.' Doherty spread his arms apart. 'This is what two generations of our people fought and died for, to let us have our jobs and families and our pints, to let us die of old age. What a shaggin great thing we have for ourselves!' Doherty took up a bottle of stout off the table and held it aloft. 'Let's hear it for old age!' The light softly wrapped itself around the brown bottle, the ooze of foam running down Doherty's fingers, disappearing around his wrists and down to his hot, hairy armpits.

The evening passed with the backdrop of the outside fury. Ambrose got up and boiled some shrimp and fish that the fishermen had sent up early in the day. The women never came near the place that night. Ambrose threw some peat into the fire, a shower of red needles disappearing up the big chimney. The draft was strong. He stood up and turned around, feeling the solitude, the coursing blood running through his head, the pulse of the temples. There was nothing more disquieting than knowing that if it wasn't for work, none of them would ever have spoken or met one another in the outside world. They would never be friends.

Doherty went over to the door and pulled it open, the wind swirling around him, the roar of the sea smashing against the rocks. A mist of spray fell lightly on the far wall. Doherty looked down at the sizzling lights in the heavy rain. The houses were indistinguishable, just the disembodied light shining uselessly in the raining night. Doherty swayed, his big belly moving as he braced the wind, the long tongue of the pier spread before him, a rampart of rock and cement. The great light turned, the slanted rain a luminous shattered glass for an instant, and then a creamy darkness again.

Ambrose looked at Doherty, a disconsolate lumbering sea creature in his great bulk, standing on fat legs, his black shoes separated like flippers. He might waddle away and slip into the darkness of the sea for ever.

'We'll see them tomorrow,' Ambrose said. 'We can play cards, what do you say?'

Ambrose felt genuinely sorry for Doherty. There they were, all alone, three men in a tub: the butcher, the baker, the candlestick maker. The sea held them prisoner at the edge of the world. Ambrose looked up into the rafters, the long shaft of the lighthouse tapering to the throb of unseen light. The entire ceiling seemed to move in a dim constellation, a hint of movement, the glimmer of parts, the great mechanical cogs turning slowly with a soft squeak, errant rays absorbed in shadows here and there in the chinks in the wooden floor above. Ambrose turned in his own sphere, another mechanism, the man machine inside the lighthouse machine. He would soon be going up in the loft beside the light, monitoring it during the night.

Doherty pushed the door shut and turned toward Ambrose. 'Let's eat something at any rate.'

The three of them ate the shrimp and fish without talking, without knowing what time it was, chewing into the rubbery meat. Doherty held the cold butter over the gas lamp to let it melt into an oily puddle in which he dipped his shrimp, then pressed the curled meat into a bed of bread and stuffed his face. The effects of the drink made him look exhausted, a man older than he was, jowls apparent when he chewed his food, the eyes small slits looking at nothing in particular as he ate. Ambrose nursed a cup of salty tea, picking the flesh off a bony mackerel. Brennan nibbled away at his meal, eating only to prove that he wasn't about to throw up, which, of course, he eventually did.

In the following weeks Ambrose had a brief fling with a girl from the town, immersing himself in Doherty's world. He wrote home about her and got nasty letters from his mother. Nothing was said directly, but she talked of finding withered flowers in her garden, an augury that things were not going well, that her son had hurt her. She sent scapulars in the post, and pictures of herself, black and white photographs that she touched up with colour crayons.

Ambrose had a pocketful of pictures which he sometimes took out on his walks, unnerved by the unabashed sexuality of the touched-up photographs, the pencilled red around the lips, the cheeks blushed, the eyebrows darkened, the teeth whitened, others of his mother in all her maternity, and the picture of his sister, eyes dotted with green crayon like an alien. What moved her to put colour into old photographs? It seemed almost sacrilegious, a conscious effort to change the past. Or was she just profoundly bored? Even on the holy pictures she sent, she touched up the wounds with red paint. Ambrose had nearly fallen victim to a sham miracle one night when he took a new scapular from an envelope and prayed with it held to his heart. He woke to find stigmatas on his chest and on the palm of his hand.

*

Every day, Brennan and Doherty watched Ambrose heading off, nodding to one another, a complicity borne more out of fear than anything else. They'd have to watch him, no doubt of that. Ambrose, conscious of them staring after him, tried to keep a stiff military posture, as though he were in pursuit of his duty, not off to go mad. Then he began sneaking out when the other two were busy making tea or looking at some charts, scampering off among the rocks for cover, moving backwards at times like a harassed crab, looking at the lighthouse as he disappeared, sometimes hearing Doherty whistling after him. 'Hey, Ambrose, come back, will you?'

On his walks, Ambrose ran the gamut: religion, sex and politics. The multiplicity of madness, the conjuring of images to counter other images, the insignificant misfit, the shy man who says great things . . . But where was the art in this litany of internal monologues, moods and feelings, if not in the art of madness commanding only himself? Murdering Brennan would have at least brought a touch of suspense and plausibility to his ways, but he couldn't bring himself to do it.

Ambrose was now stuffing envelopes with money and sending them off every week, trembling out on his walks, wondering what his mother was up to, what letter she was writing while he was out by the sea. His old affliction opened like a soft scar, and he was at it again. He knew he would be skinned at his stage with the cash he was sending his mother. There were no savings for the university. That's all he was looking for in the end, the sense of entrapment, better if it came from external forces. His mother would play her unwitting part, not that she was an innocent party in any of this when it was all said and done.

The weather grew colder. The slanted icy rains forced him to bury his head deep into his upturned collar as the ocean churned and smashed against the rocks. He could hear the sucking blowholes and the hollow clap of water shooting into the air. Clouds descended as salt drifted on the air, stinging his eyes. There was no way he could observe anything, pulled and blown around the place, the whistle of the wind, his collar crowned with rain droplets, the heavy coat sodden with moisture bending him over. There was little cover on the barren coastal road, just the lines of stony walls and the occasional tree. Ambrose pushed on toward the caves down at the beach. It was shorter than going back at this stage.

His mind turned in upon itself as he squinted his eyes. Why the hell was he out here? He'd known it was going to rain, it had been forecast. They had driven him out: Brennan and his insufferable stares. Ambrose gritted his teeth, imagining Brennan back at the lighthouse studying to get away from the pier, snug in his jumper and the bottled gas heater turned full blast to keep himself warm and Doherty going around to the pub and calling on the women, dodging showers, using it as an excuse to stop in for a chat and a cup of tea and a bit of fish at each house. How the hell could he pack that much stuff away? He told the same story from house to house, laughing and hitting his thigh at the funny parts, looking to the window and the dark clouds and nodding his head. 'What weather we're having, indeed.' That had been Doherty's people's way, going from house to house to pass on the news and get some in return.

Why couldn't he have been like that himself? Ambrose tormented himself with questions. The rain slashed about in the wind. Ambrose shouted out at the top of his voice, the tingling redness from the stinging cold rain had numbed his face and hands. He walked in a hobble, even his legs were beginning to give with the weight of water on his coat. He stopped and crouched by the wall, collapsing onto his backside, breathing hard, his head between his knees. Maybe he should turn back . . . He raked his hand through his greasy hair, the beading oiliness of his hands swollen and blue.

'I should have stayed put . . . ' he said over and over to himself. 'I should have . . . ' The rain continued. These were the days when Ambrose knew Brennan and Doherty were looking at one another and saying, 'There's trouble with him. He's not all there . . . ' And they were right! Brennan and Doherty had left their homes behind them, frantic for a better life, forcing themselves to adjust and accommodate what came their way. The three of them were making great money and had the town at their beck and call, their own little universe. They were set with food and lodging and what more could they ask for? Doherty said it that way over and over again on the nights when the storms stopped him from going down the pier to the pub.

Ambrose struggled to rise, the chatter of his teeth sending a melancholy chill down his shoulders. He pushed against the gales and rain, the sheets of rain splintering like glass on his back. He stood in his hunched manner, trying to decide which way to go now. His head was beginning to give on him, the hot and cold sweat of madness, of having said the same thing too many times. The illusion that insanity could be meted out by a sane mind was slowly dissipating. He was becoming a lunatic.

A break in the weather came on like one of his moods. The rain abated, the sky sucked up the blackness in a swirl and carried it off down the coast, and a margin of pale blue and rays of sunshine streaked across the sopping land. Ambrose looked up and saw it wouldn't last. The horizon was invisible in a mist of rain. The ocean materialized, a vicious colour smashing away on the rocks, froth floating in the air. It shared his disposed anger, at war with the land for some unknown reason, pulverizing it eternally. The wind picked up, the breeze pulling from all directions. Ambrose stopped in the muddy lane and unbuttoned his coat, releasing the heat. His coat steamed on his back and he took it off. The coolness remained in the day as he walked on breathing hard in the humid air. A tractor came around a bend, and Ambrose climbed into a ditch to let it by. The farmer saluted as he went by, five bales of hay covered in plastic on the back of the tractor.

Ambrose jumped back into the road, the lingering odour of diesel in the air. The weather was a terror for the farmers who raised cows. They had to bring up bales of dry hay when the weather went bad for a stretch and the fields turned to mud.

Ambrose walked on, the sweat cooling as he shivered and hugged himself, his shirt clinging to him. He'd been warned about this sort of thing, the hot and cold of walking in the rain. It let pneumonia creep into the lungs.

Ambrose looked back at the lighthouse set off on the edge of the pier, its stark whiteness and ring of red below the light. Brennan was in there of course. Ambrose shivered again. He might as well turn back and not die of the cold. The sky threatened more rain further up the coast and it would be dark in an hour or so anyway.

Ambrose turned and walked, the squelch of his socks in his boots bunching up and aggravating him. He stopped by the side of the road and sat down on a rock to unlace his shoes, the white crescent of his nails fumbling helplessly with the saturated laces. Ambrose roared his head off, spitting at the sky and damning everything. He finally dragged his shoes off and wrung his socks out. If he'd not been on duty he'd have walked home barefoot. As he went along there were grains of sand in his sock which cut into the withered tenderness of his feet. By the time he made it back, another shower was descending, the last rays of sunshine falling in perfect little rainbows just feet from him, the air glistening with moisture. Ambrose looked at the sea again, the steely glint of sun piercing his eyes. He turned and then it poured out of the heavens just as he reached the door of the lighthouse.

Inside, Ambrose confronted Brennan, dry as a bone, scribbling earnestly into his copybook. 'It's bad, is it?' Brennan said looking up for only a moment, absorbed in his lessons, his eyes distorted behind his thick-rimmed glasses.

'Most of the boats are docked outside . . . ' Ambrose said.

Brennan nodded, but not at what Ambrose had said. He rolled up a ball of paper in his fist and cursed.

Ambrose plodded into his room.

'Make sure you dry the floor,' Brennan said as Ambrose disappeared.

Ambrose peeled the dampness of his clothes off his hot skin. He took a stiff old towel and began to dry himself, feeling the abrasiveness of the fibres on his tender skin.

Then he came out and put his trousers, shirt and socks into the sink and wrung them dry and went to put them before the fire.

Brennan breathed hard through his nostrils and banged his fist on the table. 'Drying them is no good, I've told you that a hundred times. You have to wash them or the place will be stinking with your sour socks.'

'Do you want tea?' Ambrose said blankly, standing in his

underwear, filling the kettle.

'I do,' Brennan answered looking down again. 'I think Doherty said he was bringing up some mackerel for the dinner later.'

'That's grand,' Ambrose said, sitting down and putting his hands near the fire to warm himself.

'Just don't leave them things there,' Brennan muttered.

'Let me get warm first,' Ambrose said, feeling the heat on his palms and face as he leaned into the smoky turf.

It went this way for a long time, through the first winter and into spring, the walking around the coastal roads, climbing up the low lying hills around the area. Some days were terrible, the scowling wind hurling itself against the coast, eroding the roads, snail shells flung up onto the road crunching under his feet.

Other days were fine and breezy and Ambrose could see for miles around him, the matrix of fields and whitewashed houses dotting the coast roads. Sometimes he took a lunch with him, a few sandwiches and a flask of tea, and headed miles up the coast, climbing down into coves that nobody had stepped down into in years. He found all sorts of things washed up on these beaches, driftwood and old nets. The high walls around the cove echoed with gulls gliding on the updraft of the wind and others tucked into crevices. During the war, there had been secret plans to let the Germans land on some of these beaches, and there were other rumours of guns being sent in by U-boats to help Ireland attack England. Ambrose imagined the stealth of eyes watching him as he moved in his official uniform as though he was about the government's business and not just out to waste time.

Out on the rocks at low tide, Ambrose searched out crabs or

fish caught in pools with the low tide, watching the silent motion of the fish circling endlessly, and said to himself, 'That's just like me.'

The water took on a placid glossiness for days at a time in the summer. Families from the cities came down and began to frequent the beaches. There was a fair and boat races at which Ambrose, Brennan and Doherty were honorary judges. Ambrose decided not to go back home during the summer. The overtime was great, and he felt for a brief period when the sun shone from five in the morning until eleven at night, that maybe he could get used to this life. He exposed his white body to the sun and got himself a good tan all over as though he'd been to the Continent. Even Brennan seemed to have given up on his study for the summer, falling into a relaxed mood, sometimes going out with Ambrose on walks after dinner or going down to the pub if a musician was in for the night. Brennan explained in a simple manner what he wanted in life to Ambrose as though he were trying out new ideas. Ambrose nodded often but said little.

In late August, Ambrose got a letter from his father, saying he was cycling to see him. And he came all right one evening in his coat and hat as though he'd just come from over the hill, and not two hundred and ten miles away. His father spent all of five hours at the lighthouse, sitting with Ambrose and eating a big dish of fish, potato and cabbage.

'The land's dear enough around here?' his father asked, salting his potato.

'I never asked,' Ambrose answered, staring at his father. 'It's all old fellows holding onto what they have.'

His father shovelled the food into his mouth, mixing everything with a gulp of tea. 'I'd say they're a tough sort all right,' his father went on. 'Thick as thieves, no doubt. Are they all fishermen as well?'

Ambrose shrugged his shoulders. 'They're into nothing in particular, a bit of farming and a bit of fishing. The whole place is subsidized by the government, and a lot of the men go up across the border and draw unemployment up there as well as here.'

'By God,' Ambrose's father said, dipping his head as he took another mouthful of food. 'They're a breed apart up here. I wouldn't trust them.'

Ambrose got up and filled the kettle. Brennan was in his room reading a book, but peering over it every few minutes to look at Ambrose's father.

'How's Mam?' Ambrose asked, putting the kettle on the cooker.

His father waved his fork and knife in the air, swallowed and nodded. 'Nothing changes down with us.' He gave a jerking laugh and turned his head toward Ambrose. 'She's never done talking about you and that picture of you in your uniform is on the mantelpiece.'

Ambrose muttered, 'I didn't turn out so bad.' Ambrose looked at his father for a long time, curious to see him out of his natural habitat as it were. His father always travelled with just the clothes he had on his back, the coarse black suit, heavy overcoat and hat with a small leather bag strapped to the back of his bicycle containing a flask, some buttered bread and jam, a little package of tea leaves, a striped blue mug and a spoon. This carefully allotted ration lasted him through the long cycles in the mountains. He could stop off where he liked, situate himself beside a ditch or some cowshed, and eat quietly. Ambrose remembered times down in Limerick when his father took them off by the Shannon, his little leather bag packed with doughy sandwiches and crisps. He used to set a small fire down by the river, fill a canteen of water and boil them tea. Ambrose smiled to himself. 'Dad?'

His father looked up from his chair. 'What?'

'Do you remember that time you filled the kettle out by Plassey and when we went to drink the tea there were tiny fish floating in it?'

Ambrose's father pushed his plate from him and put his hands on the table, joining them together. 'It wasn't all bad then,' he said.

'I never said it was,' Ambrose answered softly.

There was a moment's hesitation, the wind outside picked up, rattling the windows. Ash in the grate billowed and floated in the mellow daylight, a grainy static. They were fettered together for a brief moment in the confines of the lighthouse, the threaded memory of past times uncoiled by this long hard cycle. Unconsciously his father must have planned of this journey and its outcome, but only ever felt the conscious urge to get on his bicycle and start peddling. The rest would unfold without effort. He had this way without words, an instinctive simplicity of purpose. He proved himself in deeds, not words. Ambrose steadied himself, holding the back of a chair, looking at his father, knowing that he should say nothing, that nothing was being demanded of him.

'I'll have more tea,' his father finally said.

'Right,' Ambrose answered, snapping out of his daze.

Ambrose's father reached into his pocket and took out a small medal with a glass encase in the centre of it. 'It's a bit of bone, a relic of some eejit. She had it blessed up at St Joseph's for you.'

Ambrose set another cup of tea down before his father and took the medal. The small pearly fragment was set against a ruby backdrop, highlighting the blanched bone.

His father brought the tea to his lips and drank. Then he put the cup down and stood up. Sitting had begun to stiffen his aging limbs. He rubbed his lower back with his big thumbs, uncharacteristically wincing and actually twisting his torso in a circular motion over his hips. He had to put one hand on his hat as he turned a second time. 'I'll be off then,' he said.

Ambrose furrowed his brow. 'But you only got here. Aren't you going to stay for a few days? We have room and tomorrow I'll show you up along the coast. There's great beaches.'

His father straightened himself, his face flushed with the rush of blood to his head. 'What would I want with a beach? I'll push on. There's a couple of things that need doing back home.'

Brennan came out with his book in his hand, looking down the few steps from his bedroom into the main room. 'You're not leaving?' He had a sly smile, and winked at Ambrose as if to say, 'So this is where the madness comes from.'

Ambrose's father could be pulled into nothing. He drank the dregs of tea without looking up, banged the mug down and wiped his sleeve across his mouth. 'That was grand, Ambrose.'

'I'll walk you out then.'

'Where's the toilet?'

Ambrose and Brennan stood looking at one another as Ambrose's father disappeared. 'How long did it take him to get here?' Brennan said. He had his book open, flat against his waist.

Ambrose shook his head. 'I don't know.'

His father appeared again in his hat and coat and put a strong

108

lean arm around Brennan like a vice. 'Best of luck, now.'

'Dad, there's a bit of fish and potato here for you that I've packed.'

'Lovely. Now you're talking.' His father moved on bandy bicycle legs.

At the end of the pier Ambrose took an envelope out of his pocket and put it into his father's hand. His father leaned the bicycle up against the wall. 'I know this isn't what you wanted.'

Ambrose puffed up his face, holding back the tears. 'I'm working with the government. What could be better than that?'

'As you will, son.' His father released his grip and sat down on a rock, took off his shoe and sock and put the envelope into the sock and then put the sock and shoe on again. He stood up and shook his leg out. 'We'll be seeing you at Christmas anyway. I have a couple of pigs that are about to litter and we'll be set. This,' and his father pointed to his shoe, 'is only a loan.' He said it with such conviction, as though he'd said it over and over again on the way up on the bicycle.

Ambrose nodded. 'Mind yourself, Dad.'

His father was on his bicycle, his legs straddling the crossbar. 'Don't worry. It's all downhill on the way back,' and then he turned the pedal and sat on the big leather seat and off he went. Four hundred and twenty miles in two days on an old kip of a bicycle without any gears. Ambrose stood and watched his father lean into the sharp rise of the mountains.

A few weeks later the sky broke in early October. Nobody came down to the village once this sort of weather set in, the hills in the surrounding area frosted and were treacherous to motorists.

The same old antics with Brennan started again and Ambrose took to the roads once more. His routine was observed by the town's people. They spoke among themselves about where and when they saw Ambrose. He was out in sheds during sleet and snow, looking gravely at empty fields. The stories became so out of hand, that sometimes three different people would come in with stories of having just seen Ambrose in three different places separated by miles of fields.

For Ambrose's part, he was playing a waiting game until Christmas, or that was what he told himself. If he could just last that long. Thank God there were such things as Holy Holidays. Ambrose felt the affliction of his father's visit on him for a long time. Coming that distance to sit with him for just a few hours, what kind of man was he? Ambrose spent time watching the farmers in the district, listening to a dog's hollow bark in a cold hallway off in the distance, the smell of turf in the air. He stopped outside other small houses, staring in the windows at old men sitting down by their own fires. This had been his father's way, the loneliness of the kitchen, the dark hours where he sat without light, with his head on the table sleeping in his hat and coat.

If a dog acted up and started barking, Ambrose would have to go into the small cottages and sit for a few minutes and ask some stupid questions about activity in the area, pretending to write notes down in a book.

Most of the farmers were old men in black suits who had lived through the Civil War and the great wars. The time of revolutions had passed for now. They had worked their small plots of land, raising cows and pigs, if not oblivious to, then untouched by the misery of what they heard by word of mouth or on the radio. Ambrose could see it in their eyes as he walked by the farm gates, nodding and returning nods in mute animal acknowledgment. Ambrose sat in with them, thinking how this was what his father had wanted, an inheritance of land and animals, his own domain.

Ambrose had a steadfastly romantic vision of these poor men. The sanity of provincialism, potato eaters with one foot on the spade and their hearts with God, bony men, resurrected from the famine. He often asked himself if he actually believed any of it.

Ambrose pressed on during the cold months. The pain had begun. The clarity of his grievances was convoluted in a need to appropriate and comment on everything. He had time to draw things out to absurdity. He thought of himself wrapped up in the schizophrenia of his own country, a man looking to fit himself into the world.

Ambrose found a small cave down by the beach, a refuge from the wind and rain. This became his haunt for hours on end each day while the sickness matured. Ambrose entered at low tide, climbing up a rampart of slimy, dark green algae-covered rocks to sit alone as the sea came in slowly until he was marooned in its mouth, a dark figure in a heavy coat, a piece of a jigsaw puzzle staring at the sea frothing and crashing on the rocks in the bay. Sometimes he put his head down on a flat stone and curled up and tried to sleep, his hands in his crotch to keep himself warm. The Civil Service examination had brought him to the edge of the world, to a cave on a remote lighthouse outpost. The vacuous days, the pounding waves, the constant turning light never ceased to affect him, the constant motor of life repeated day and night, night and day and on and on and him rising and working and walking and then sleeping, then rising, working, walking, ad infinitum. Should that have brought him to boredom? It gave him at least security, and couldn't he have coped with boredom for the sake of security? Did boredom not also haunt those in poverty and hunger? Maybe the farmers were really looking out at the sea, imagining the lives of brothers and sisters who left them years ago for America and Australia. Maybe they were grieving the prisoner's solitude he felt at the lighthouse. All that differed was that they owned their land. Did owning something provide that much sanity?

Ambrose found the cave exactly what he was after. If he were going to change, it should have been from some place of symbolism, the intellectual in the cave of the prehistoric. He would rid himself of the mire and psychoses of his past years, leave Ireland and enroll himself at a university in England. He sat alone staring at seashells, picking some up in his hand, probing the soft creatures curled inside, the timid flesh curling from his curious finger. He felt sure life had started in this crude form, unemotional cells out in the oceans. He tapped a shell on the rock, breaking it open, scooping out the small, slimy snail, pinching it between his fingers. This is what he and all things had evolved from. It seemed absurd, himself and the snail, brothers from a time when all things lived in the oceans, the common ancestor of cows and dogs and man, all land breathers who had abandoned their place of creation. Cows were fish who gave milk, dogs, fish who barked, man, a fish with a bicycle. Ambrose strained over, dipping the snail into a puddle of water, tiny creatures skimming on the surface and beneath. He had been achieved by a tide of sperm, a frantic swim in darkness. He was the product of a good swimming sperm, a gestation inside the shiny sack of another world of water, the snorkel of his belly button breathing for him, and those months of nursing, suckling into the vast tides of fluids, wells of milk. He let the snail plop into the puddle and raised his head. Here he was, a creature so alienated from the medium of his birth that he could not even swim.

Ambrose brought sandwiches out to the cave, and a flask of tea as the days went on, to keep himself in health. But for all his provisions, over a period of a month he developed a lingering cold and a persistent cough.

One evening the sea pounded the beach so hard that he could not get out of the cave and had to spend the night shivering and blowing into his hands until the sea subsided. He struggled home, blue and frozen. Doherty had the sailors looking for Ambrose. He'd been afraid Ambrose had tried to drown himself.

Ambrose shrugged off questions, materializing back at the door of the lighthouse without the energy to open it, his hands numbed by the cold rain. He stayed in his room, missing his shift under the pretext of illness. His lungs were badly congested, and he spat up bloody phlegm into a bucket by his bed. He only came out when Doherty left at night for the pubs, creeping out, dressed up in his dishevelled uniform which was creased and filthy and missing some buttons. Brennan was ever-present at the table, the naked bulb like a bright idea beside his head. He engrossed himself in the accounting books, his rimmed glasses snug on his face so that when he looked up his eyes were magnified.

Ambrose said nothing, huddling his arms around his body, as he boiled a pot of water to mix in a powder for his cold, and then went back across the cold floor and slipped into his bed, unable to sleep. He had destroyed his health for no good reason. He hadn't the ability to understand anything beyond the forces that impinged on him, like that snail in the cave. And that constituted nothing, a crude animal discomfort.

The still spider-web silence of the long days passed, the hum of the lighthouse turning in its finite universe, the sucking water outside meeting the horizon. On the days of sunlight, a pendulum of shadows moved in slow motion across the floor. He heard the wood breathing with warmth, expanding and creaking, earwigs scurrying in and out of peppered holes. Then darkness set, dissolving colour into bleakness, a light of nuances, of shapes, and still he had his eyes wide open.

Neither Doherty nor Brennan wanted to interfere in the situation, to bring out the authorities. They were well set in their ways, making a life for themselves. They didn't want a new man to be commissioned to the lighthouse and see what they were doing. It was better that Ambrose sorted himself out alone. They just hoped that they could get what they needed accomplished before Ambrose finally went mad.

Ambrose's cold broke eventually, but he was left shaken. He'd lost over a stone in weight. He was the image of a scarecrow as he moved in the oversized black suit. Now, where was he to go? His reputation with the people had become so bad that nobody dared to come up and bring him something. The fishermen didn't want their daughters ending up with a banjaxed lunatic.

The hope of university was gone. What Ambrose needed now was an event to break the monotony of useless drivel that occupied his head. He had to get away from the lighthouse at all costs, even he knew that, but could he just pack it in like that? Once he resigned, he would never be accepted again, and what else was there? Maybe he could just pretend he'd gone mad. In fact, he wasn't sure if he could pretend otherwise.

The fever of the cold had brought on the weight loss. He had not consciously starved or denied himself food, but he had denied his brain sustenance. Ambrose began his convalescence by trying to get out and get some air, eating down at the local chipper some days, a cod and chips, or a fry for breakfast other days. He knew the people were staring at him dressed up in his filthy uniform, his face with days of growth, his hair uncombed. He smelt of illness, secreting a bittersweet odour of days of lying without bathing mixed with the grease from the chippers which had become ingrained in his skin. His case was now the talk of the village. Still, Ambrose wanted to roar his head off. He wanted to go down to the lighthouse, wash himself up and leave during the night for England. He got up and half-walked, half-ran back to the lighthouse, but then collapsed and slept for what he was later told was two days. He awoke and looked in his savings book. There was 400 pound which would set him up for two months or so in England. Yes, he was going to leave all this behind once and for all. What he had to do now was concentrate on eating solidly.

That's what he would do then. It was settled. Ambrose nodded his head, speaking to himself. But first he would sleep. He needed rest and set himself down and closed his eyes, and then he was up and sitting on the edge of the bed. He could not quit his job. There was nothing else for him. What would his mother think? The blight of disaffection persisted. He fought with himself about his lack of courage over the next week, and all the while he kept stuffing so much money into the envelopes for his mother that he finally had only 78 pound in his savings account when he checked a week later. That ended any immediate hope of escape to England.

Madness for Ambrose did not preclude a tacit understanding of the world around him, even if he did not fully understand his own actions. Without money, he was trapped. And what would escape do for him? He still wanted to know what had happened to himself. Ambrose was simple in that regard, a creature irresistibly allied to cause and effect, who felt that guilt had to have its motivation in sin. But what sin could he find? A clinical illness of self-doubt not prompted by cursing or murder . . . Where was the sin? He was a saint by any standard, a man who gave money to his family. Yes, 'The meek shall inherit the earth.' It was in the Scriptures.

Doherty grew scared of the situation. He thought it would be best to call in someone while Ambrose was on the upswing, when the effects of the cold were still apparent. Maybe Ambrose was coming down with tuberculosis. Doherty didn't want to be accused of letting Ambrose get this bad. He began dressing up in his uniform every morning and cleaned up the lighthouse. If there was going to be trouble, he wanted to be in the clear.

Ambrose watched him and sensed that the end was at hand. Doherty brought him tea and toast and a few books he'd been given by a brother who had gone to university. 'You might as well take a look at these,' Doherty said while he sat on a chair and read the newspaper, pretending that the extent of Ambrose's problems was all due to the persistence of the cold he had caught. Doherty made up some excuse for spending time with Ambrose, but put it down to genuine concern. Ambrose dabbled in the different books, reading bits and pieces of chapters. In the end he could never keep the stories straight, mixing up characters and places. He lingered in Doherty's deception, admiring how tenaciously Doherty clung to his own mission. He called him 'Florence Nightingale' and tried to show that he was no fool, but Doherty persisted in bringing in tea and toast while he watched Ambrose eat in bed.

Brennan came in one evening while Doherty was in with Ambrose. He was taking a break from the tedious hours of study, rubbing a pain in his lower back. 'Maybe you should take a weekend home,' Brennan said with blank candour, going over to the window and staring out at the darkness. The night was freezing. Ambrose's room was permeated with the dampness, the cold stone wet to the touch. Brennan shivered. 'You'll never get over this cold in this place. There's bad weather forecast for the rest of the week.'

Doherty looked up from the paper and nodded his head, venturing into the conversation slowly. The coldness affected his stomach. He was always passing gas from inhaling the cold air, and the effects of the years of drinking were finally catching up with him. 'That would do you good, Ambrose. You can't live on tea and toast. You have a week's holiday coming to you. Take it and go away for a bit.' Doherty had his legs crossed, the paper folded up on his lap.

Ambrose could not bring himself to speak and feigned tiredness, his eyes moving languidly in their sockets. Brennan put his thin face over Ambrose and looked down on him. 'You look sick. Jesus Christ, if you keep this up, you'll get TB, do you hear me?'

Ambrose looked up vacantly, wrapped in the heavy blankets on the bed. They wanted him to go and leave them alone. This was an ultimatum. He almost envied the simplicity of these men, the firmness of their convictions passing as common sense. Ambrose lay on his back, the tea and toast getting cold, untouched on the three-legged table. He had developed a rash on the left side of his face. His breath smelt acrid. His lips were dried and cut. And for what and why? Still the illusive moral machine in his head turned, demanding a real crisis, some legitimate stimulus that would justify the obliterating pain and shame that seethed in his head. He had that much moral scruple. He could not do something without being able to say, 'I did it because this man or this woman did this to me.' But he was denied it. He believed in absolutely nothing outside the realm of his home, outside the district of his birth. He had done nothing wrong in his whole life, a guiltless man, a charitable man, a sick man. For Ambrose there had been no crime, only punishment. His sin now was the inability to make up a crime, or the lack of volition to go out and do something desperate. His sin was a lack of imagination. His head lived outside of experience. His mind settled on his mother in his poignant moments of real despair, and he saw her looking at him, speaking about her faith in him, and how he was under her religious spell, moved and prodded by faith, and he believed that, to some extent, and also that the moment he went up to Dublin after her bawling her head off and sat down and took the Civil Service examination he had set himself up to be a martyr.

'Well, what is it going to be?' Brennan insisted. He was still staring down at Ambrose. Brennan needed some more months of peace and quiet to get his studies completed.

Ambrose became conscious that an answer was being demanded of him. He answered in a toneless voice, 'I might go home for the weekend.' It was a voice that fooled nobody.

But Doherty stood up, set the paper aside and rubbed his hands together, relieved to have something said. He didn't care about deception or causes, only the effect of what was achieved. 'Now we're talking,' Doherty shouted. 'A long weekend with the family, a hot meal and a nice fire will do you a world of good. I'll arrange for a ticket for you, Ambrose. You'll be over this cold and be right as rain in no time flat. A change of scenery will do you a world of good.' The tips of Doherty's ears and his nose turned a deep scarlet when he grew excited.

'You're right, Doherty,' Ambrose said, 'I'll be right as rain in no time.' Ambrose smiled and showed his pink gums and the protrusion of his yellowing teeth.

The two men left the room in single file, the apprentice accountant and the man in search of a wife, Doherty with the untouched tea and toast balanced in his hands, Brennan holding the door for him and then closing it, grunting something under his breath. Had it come to this? Jesus, Ambrose wanted to roar his head off, run out and dive at Brennan and smash his head. Doherty he could at least understand, but Brennan, trying to force Ambrose out of the lighthouse, and all so he could study and earn money. Ambrose found the volition to curse at the top of his lungs. Christ! The psychoanalytic minds of those two, standing before him, the tea and toast there for him, trying to oust him from the end of the pier. He had heard of taking a long walk off a short pier, but to stop and live at the end of the pier, blasted by storms, hidden in mists, the three of them, all frustrated men set together in a great phallus with a throbbing light on top . . . Wasn't it absurd enough to drive him insane?

But Ambrose did not deal in irony now, or metaphor. He calmed down. The long chain of emotion had spun itself out until he was left with abstraction again. He stared at the ceiling as the sea whispered through the porthole window, a wet eye, longing for those great days of being the Tea Boy to a fat, aging mother, putting himself before her in all his servile ways, letting her know that she was responsible for bringing him into the world.

Of course, Ambrose was going to say none of that. Just to be near her, that was his goal, to look at her with the seductiveness of mental illness, in the way that only the truly sick can. As he lay sweating on the bed, Ambrose knew that Doherty was right, and Brennan had seen it all along. Ambrose was a man who needed to be with his mother, whatever the hell you called that. It was an obsession, a possession, not carnal as much as ontological. To harass her, not so much by words as by osmosis, sending her his hate and dissatisfaction through the pores in his body. He would be there in what he called 'Indecent Composure' with a water bottle for her, a cup of tea at her waking and sleeping, whispering into her dreams how much it meant to be with her, the machine of his birth.

Ambrose did not go home. He spent the next few days trying to drag himself out of the morass into which he had put himself. Even if he went home, he'd have to have some more money in his account. Doherty offered to lend him some, but Ambrose refused. He would leave when the time was right, and he thanked Doherty profusely for the tea and toast. Ambrose sent his uniform out with a man who came down to collect the fish for a restaurant in the city and had it dry cleaned. If the other two could cope with life, well, so could he. The optimism of a new resolve brought him out of his dourness. He attributed all his troubles to the cold. The whim of sickness brought on these sudden moments of exuberance where he pushed one mood aside for another, embracing some idea unequivocally. He still believed he was alive for some purpose. He would not give up. He had lain like a rock, immobile, and still the torment had plagued him. He would do as his father had done before him, work himself hard, deprive himself of the ability to think, absorb himself in the job.

Ambrose came out of his room and bought medicine down at the chemist's and set his mind on getting well. At lunch times, he made an appearance on the pier, walking down to the edge of the town, nodding with as much dignity as he could muster. His appetite was still flagging, but he forced himself to eat some fish. The exercise brought colour back to his face. Maybe he would send off to the university in England and do a course by correspondence. That wouldn't take up much of his money, and he'd have his time occupied.

It seemed that the crisis might have passed. Ambrose was sitting in the main room across from Brennan, writing to his mother, when a letter arrived. He didn't recognize the handwriting at all, but it was postmarked Limerick.

His father thanked Ambrose for what he was doing for his brother. Desmond was doing well at the university. Ambrose was doing a great thing for his brother. His father had wanted to tell him back in August when he came to see him, but it didn't seem like the right time to say anything. Ambrose's father went on and asked at the end of the letter, 'Would you still like to be an architect?'

Ambrose sat at the wooden table, his log book open, the tedium of his days recorded by hour and day. He was numb, paging through days, tides, sunrises, sunsets, temperatures, pressures, cloud cover, things he did not care about. Then he shut the book. He stared at the wooden table, at the carved initials of the men who had worked at the end of the pier, men who had moved on from this outpost. Then he got up and went to the toilet and vomited on his knees. Christ, his own brother, that fat figure who had worked silently without help all those years was at the university with Ambrose's own money!

Brennan got up and hid his books, fearing that Ambrose was gone mad again. He never heard such roaring.

Doherty came in, laughing in the company of two fishermen, and saw the look on Brennan's face. Brennan stood by the gas heater and pointed at the toilet door.

Ambrose shook, holding the wooden toilet seat, unable to move, vomiting into the small neck of the toilet, the rush of salty seawater lapping down at the end of the dark funnel.

'What did you say to him?' Doherty snarled at Brennan. He was half-drunk, cocking his head back in a menacing way. The brilliance of cool sunlight poured in behind Doherty.

'Nothing! Don't you touch me, Doherty.' Brennan stood his ground, taking off his glasses.

'I wouldn't waste my time.' Doherty found Ambrose. He got the two fishermen to take a hold of him and carry him into bed.

Brennan looked at Doherty. 'You should have sent him home a long time ago.'

'Is he sick?' one of the fishermen said.

Doherty glared at Brennan. 'You must have said something to him!'

Brennan persisted. 'You should have sent him home. He's gone mad. You were in charge here, not me.'

Doherty found the letter and read it and understood. 'I'll deal with this tomorrow,' Doherty said to Brennan. 'Open University is over for you, Brennan. Just wait until the Commissioner comes down here and sees what's been going on.' Then Doherty left with the fishermen.

'Just try it,' Brennan shouted. 'You're as much in everything as I am.'

The following morning, Doherty went up the town and called the Department and said Ambrose was suffering from a very bad cold and had gone delirious.

When the officials came down, Ambrose had left the lighthouse. They eventually found him sitting with his legs tightly tucked against his chest in the cave. It was the only way he could keep his legs from shaking. He got up quietly when they found him. 'That fuckin whore,' was all he said to Doherty, his eyes wet and jaded from the lack of sleep.

Doherty put his hand on Ambrose's shoulder, helping him across the beach, the sand getting into his shoes. Doherty had been sending money home since he left as well. He understood the burden of a poor family.

'I'm going to get her back, though,' Ambrose whispered, leaning on Doherty. Out in the cave, he had taken a vow of celibacy. 'I'm going to live with her for the rest of her days.' He did not have the courage to kill himself. For all his remaining days he would live by the dogged fatalism that someday in the future these cushy jobs would end, and what then for the offspring of this new class of contented middle-class religious? The vapid contentment of one generation would be replaced by the vicious competition of too many creatures in pursuit of the same end.

Ambrose's days would be forever filled with that clairvoyant truth, sitting in the presence of his mother, bringing her tea to her chair, the finite provincialism re-established, listening to her go on about her sham miracles – at least she had her delusions – nodding his head with quivering patience, his tongue hanging from his mouth, 'Yes Mam, this and yes Mam, that,' ordaining ordinary life as her miracles, his eyes always watching the sky for the first flash of destruction, waiting to take a poker before the end and at least have the solace of killing her.

The three government officials walked slowly across the beach, looking at one another like men at a funeral. On the following day, Brennan asked to be reassigned. Only Doherty remained on duty on the pier. He married one of the local girls and began a family. The last time Ambrose checked, he had six girls and two boys.

Ambrose entered hospital for treatment, and they poured electricity into his skull, all things coming together in lucid moments of awareness as they hooked him up to the machine. The finite economy of the universe, the fragments gathered together again. The soft rubber ball placed in his mouth could have been the ball from the handball alley from his school days, having hopped uselessly for all those years until finding its way into his gob for this auspicious occasion. And the jolt of electricity had been there all along too, an inheritance from his father, the supreme checks and balances of Newtonian physics, 'for every action there is an equal and opposite reaction', a pure moral physics adaptable to all forces, his father burning off the electricity of his distress on his bicycle, the flickering dynamo of energy spent, and now at the end of it all, the electricity found its way back into the padded walls of a hospital, years out of time, an errant force now channelled into Ambrose's head to complete its circuit.

The Civil Service kept Ambrose's job for him, 'civil' to the end. He was stationed down in his home town with the local Department of Fisheries office. Sometimes Ambrose felt that, despite everything, maybe he was the luckiest man alive. His madness would be paid for by the state for all of his natural life.

Years had passed in and out of the institution up in Dublin, punctuated by periods of blackness after the shock treatments. Ambrose stayed with his parents, civil and silent, a silent Civil Servant, a silent, nonviolent Civil Servant. There was no losing his job down in Limerick despite the trips to the institution. Ambrose had been right on that point anyway. At least his theory of socialism was standing the test of time. The great dream of hire-purchase had come of age with the first washing machines and convection ovens, the high shag carpet and built-in kitchen units. Big families of churchgoers were cropping up all over the place. The great beeding frenzy was in full swing in the new wave of small three-bedroom housing estates. The amount of sex going on in these estates boggled Ambrose's mind. Sex and commerce must have had a direct correlation. The prospect of marriage had vanished for Ambrose. Who would want a demented man? The awareness of sex happening all around him as he walked through the estates brought him to a new obsession.

Exercise was part of Ambrose's recuperation. He was told to take up walking. The drugs would bring on a lethargy which he had to fight. A solid routine had been prescribed.

Ambrose had his walks charted out. The long walks around the city helped him lose the weight he'd gained during his stays at the hospital. He took most of his walks late at night. He passed house after house and knew exactly what was going on, lights on up in bedrooms, the shadowy figures moving around, copulation concealed only forty feet from where he stood. He was persecuted by erections as he walked along, stopping from time to time with his hands buried in his pockets, looking up at the small enclosures of 12 feet by 15 feet rooms, smelling of new paint and dry oil-furnace heat, slippers bashful under the new beds. Ambrose felt his leg twitch, his pelvis contract. His nose sniffed the cold air.

The estates were all mortgaged on a dream, people enjoying life in the present, paying in the future. It was all based on compound interest. Such a novel idea, a profundity that could not be understood but merely lived by ordinary people. Ambrose looked around him. People with as much or as little brains as himself were living in these houses. He could have moved into one of those places, maybe he still could. Could he move beyond the past and enter into this strange new present?

Ambrose had an acute awareness that the very idea of time had changed, a psychological displacement as radical as Copernicus and his heliocentric universe or Einstein and his $E=mc^2$. Here, a new law of time had been invented, something unnatural. The future had been incorporated into the present. The past had been discarded. Who and what your people were did not matter out here. This was an estate built outside the city in a cow pasture. A ubiquitous egalitarianism prevailed. What seemed important was that this small oasis of young people set apart would reproduce and consume, breed offspring to continue the cycle and move into new estates and have their own offspring who would continue in wants, ad infinitum. It seemed so elemental as Ambrose walked around the estates like a policeman on his rounds, his hands behind his back, his lips muttering away. This sort of vision, this sanitized uniformity had its attraction. Maybe he was scoffing at the spectacle only because his hope of meeting a woman to share it seemed dim. These estates had a simple organic intent, a circular pattern of saving and spending, a living bank ledger. As Ambrose said to himself, man had given up a Higher God for Hire-Purchase.

Ambrose liked to think in these terms. He'd given up on reality for the time being. The absurdity of abstraction held less pain for him. It was all useless drivel that entered and left his head. It was a far cry from the days in the hotel when the first salesmen came to the old houses and sprinkled dirt on a carpet and then sucked it up like magic with Hoovers and tried to convince people that they would one day be unable to live without the alien contraptions they were peddling. Even Ambrose had been a sceptic in those years. But new gadgets for a new generation.

Ambrose had been trying to reconceptualize his illness as some short-fused circuit since his last trip to the institution. He'd abandoned religion entirely. He'd become a disciple of pain, submitting to the shock treatment. It was so much easier to speak of chemical imbalance than of half-truths about things that had happened in his childhood.

The current of electricity had seared deep inside him, filling him with a tingling feeling for weeks and months. The hair on his arms and legs stood on end sometimes when he thought about it, the mild buzz of energy still pulsing deep within his cells. They had spoken in such clinical terms around him when all he had wanted to talk about was his mother. But they had explained that his mother had nothing to do with it.

The mystery of insanity was taken away from him. All his antics could be traced to misfiring synapses in the right dorsal lobe. They had plastic models which came apart where they showed him where things had gone wrong. They put a pin into his skull to scrape at the brain, as though it was a blackboard that could be erased. It had worked on mice. 'On mice who hated their mother?' Ambrose asked. 'No, mice who got lost in a maze.'

Still, Ambrose submitted to this treatment, this brave new science. He was taking what he called capsule mathematics, five kinds of tablets, neuron inhibitors which could stop him shaking and saying things like 'that fuckin ol' whore', which really was a great medical feat. Of course no mouse ever said that. Ambrose began to understand that the metaphor of his language really said, 'I am a mouse lost in a maze.'

Where to go from here? The city off in the distance, the spiralling cathedrals looming toward heaven, the cluster of lights sprinkled here and there, the margins of blackness and then light. He walked onward every night with his hands in his coat. When it rained hard he went into a bus shelter, the road glossed with the sheen of light on water. There wouldn't be a bus for ages at this hour. He was halfway between the world of mathematics and the world of superstition, the world of dark alleys and slaughter, of profound violence, men without jobs, women without hope, the grimy layer of coal soot resting on everything and making it black down in the city. This was where he'd been formed, in the myth of his mother's religion, a prayer answered. He stood shaking on these nights in the cold, the duality of two hemispheres always apparent before him. Why could he not live in one dimension, why did he have to be the interloper, occupying the grey matter of two husks of influence, feeling both, understanding neither? Finally a bus would come lumbering around a corner and pull up in the rain, and Ambrose would fish around in his pocket for his free travel pass, courtesy of the Department of Health, and sit down, and the bus would rumble into town.

Still, Ambrose was occupying more of the rational world than he had done in the past despite his apparent lapses. The job saw to that to some extent. The rovings on the road were punctuated by greater periods of sobriety. Even his hatred of his mother abated for a time, with his father around the house and all that. It may have been the shock treatment, or the pills, or maybe Ambrose had finally found contentment, a bachelor with a roof over his head and a hot meal in his stomach. After all, he was back in the place of his birth with a grand job. How many men could say they got what they wanted all their lives? There was the slight complication of mental illness, but sure he'd cope. This was planet earth, not heaven. His problem seemed solved for the time being as long as he followed his doctor's orders.

Being a mental patient was a great luxury, really, and the more people knew of Ambrose's apparent illness, the less was asked of him. Ambrose called it a law of diminishing returns: give him something and he gave back less. Consequently, he did next to nothing. He could show up to work whenever he wanted, and nobody said a word against him. He had medical papers from a higher authority: the Department of Health. He slept late into the morning. He said to himself, if not suicide, then sleep. He rose at his own leisure and did what he pleased, taking out the ashes from the grate in the sitting room and then heading up toward work for a cup of tea and a walk along the docks to relax himself and get some exercise. His job was to ensure that all the relevant Department rules and regulations were observed. Often he accompanied the customs officials who searched the vessels for illegal materials, supplies of pornographic magazines, condoms and sexual gadgets. They'd been commissioned as a moral watchdog for the Limerick area. Ambrose thought that was a great laugh.

The routine continued through the years, in and out of hospital, off to work and then off down home on his bicycle and back into bed in his uniform for a bit of television or the papers and then a deep sleep, then up at nights and back to the docks. All variants of the same old thing: wasting time. Slothfulness had always been a penchant of his. He sometimes rotated this routine three times a day or night, depending upon which shift he was supposedly working.

Despite the ironic humour Ambrose took from having a job while remaining a certified schizophrenic, a sense of numbness prevailed. He tucked into big feeds of potatoes and meat in the interim, swallowing tablets with each meal, keeping everything at bay. Eating had become his only solace, huge amounts of food shovelled into himself. It induced sleep sometimes. On rainy days he stood around in the hallway, pacing back and forth, deciding if he should go up to bed or keep walking off the nervousness in his body.

His mother would be in the sitting room drifting in and out of sleep after the midday dinner. Even his father had begun to slow down with the years. He would sit at the kitchen table paging through the newspaper slowly, not bothering with Ambrose, a cup of tea at his elbow. Limerick wallowed in this twilight existence, the old air-raid siren wailing through the city, the long lunch in the mid-afternoon, Kerry Pinks mashed with milk, a slab of salty ribs, marrow fat peas steeped since the day before, a little custard and rhubarb or apple pie for dessert and a cup of tea to wash it down. The wireless beeped for the one o'clock news, listened to with reverent silence by the man of the house. It was a great life if you could stand it. Ambrose always felt he could have managed it, but now the twitch of nervousness began in his legs and ran up his body to his face when he was trapped like this for hours in the house.

The absolute vocation to boredom could have gone on like this for ever, and nothing short of the death of either of his parents, or his own of course, could have changed it. And indeed, it was sickness that brought about the change. Ambrose was in the hospital for the Christmas holidays treating himself to what he called 'the National Health Hotel'. The time in hospital had extended into a three-month session. Then the news came that his father was sick. At first he thought it was a dream. Then he got out of bed and answered a telephone call from Limerick down in the long corridor. 'Is it bad? It's not. Well, maybe I should come all the same?'

The voice on the other end of the phone was filled with static. Ambrose could barely hear what was being said.

'All the best now,' Ambrose said into the black receiver and put it down.

Ambrose stood in the long corridor. He'd let them keep him too long at the institution. Things would change once more. The dour lull that his aging father had set down at the house would soon lift. What he was afraid of was that his mother would have the house out from under him and escape herself and leave him banjaxed for the rest of his life down in Limerick. She was on for an easy time anywhere she could get it. If she sold the house she could choose between her beleaguered children, offering them the money from the house to take her in for ever.

Now he might lose her and the house. He shouldn't have been gone so long, let a situation like this evolve where she could get the upper hand. Ambrose banged the glass in the phone booth. He knew if his brother was calling him at the institution that something serious had happened. They were priming him for something bigger. Well, by Jasus, he was going to get down as fast as he could and stake his claim on his mother. She wouldn't leave Limerick if he had his way, and there was nobody who could really stop him when he wanted his way. He went up to his room and began packing. He'd been playing a mediocre second-division madness these past years, dabbling in finger-painting and basket weaving at the hospital, telling menacing stories about his inhibitions to the doctors to whittle away the time, but he was ready to step up a notch. There were a couple of words left unsaid with his mother which were not going to go unsaid much longer, no matter how much basket weaving and painting he did. Ambrose could paint away to sublimate a condition, but he held his old friend the poker in great regard.

Ambrose grinned and rubbed his hands together as he packed up his tricks. Thank God, he had a job waiting for him at home.

In the morning he requested an interview with his doctor and expressed concern for his father's condition, and gave a good account of his own, deeming himself well enough to resume his work at the docks.

The doctor obliged and signed him out, which was really a formality as Ambrose was no sociopath, suffering only a clinical form of mild schizophrenia, something that could probably have been cured by a sound marriage or a kick in the arse, as he said himself. One of those borderline cases. Still, Ambrose wasn't complaining. He occupied two worlds, the land of the sane and the insane. He could go where he pleased, check in and check out at his own convenience, plead sanity or insanity by his own decree. Two persons in one body.

Ambrose went down the long entrance by the grazing cows toward the bus stop. Outside the gates of the institution, he boarded a bus for the city centre to get the connection to the train. He lugged his bags after him down the narrow passage of the bus, up the narrow stairs and plunked down into a seat, cursing. The upper deck of the bus filled with people whispering to one another. Ambrose fidgeted with his luggage at his side. A haze of smoke hung in the bus, the windows misted with condensation, other people's breath.

Christ, he should have ordered a taxi to the station. The bus harboured germs for every sort of illness, people coughing and sneezing. Ambrose tried to hold his breath as someone sniffled behind him.

He wiped the glass with his tie and stared out the window. The day was freezing, not the kind of day to leave a hospital. Already he felt the fatigue besieging his body. The games he pursued in his mind, in the institution or at home, lifted when he was out among people. It would take him all his time to foist some abstract theories on life as the bus moved him toward his destination.

A fat man in an anorak with artificial fur around the edge of the hood sank down beside Ambrose and hemmed him into the window. Ambrose pressed his face up against the cold glass. Jesus, he couldn't believe it. The teeming glass, the condensed breath of these germ-bearing creatures around him. Ambrose put his hand to his face, trying to stifle the dank odour. His stomach convulsed and he thought he was going to vomit.

'What a fuckin disaster up North, know what I mean?' The fat man elbowed Ambrose. 'How's it goin there?' The fat man had a large round childish face with small little eyes and a tiny mouth as though his head had expanded but his features had not grown. He saw the case beside Ambrose. 'Goin on holidays, is it? Lucky for some.'

'Right,' Ambrose said, and drew himself into his coat and continued to stare out the window into the yards of houses, watching clothes hanging on the lines. He could see people sitting at kitchen tables. His eyes strained to catch every detail. He needed to shift his attention to something that would ease his head.

The fat man belched and pinched his nostrils, breathing hard, his body swelling and then deflating. He played with the zipper on his anorak, looking around for someone to harass. 'Mornin,' he said in his thick accent to people huddled up in their seats. Ambrose didn't turn, but he heard the reluctant responses. 'Morning . . . How're ya . . . How's the form?'

'Can't complain, but listen til I tell ya. Did ya see the telly last night? Such a shower of fuckers up North!' The fat man touched the man in front of him and said, 'Honest to God, what a disaster. Hi, mister, is that this morning's paper?' The fat man laughed to himself. 'That's not the *Irish Times*, boss, is it?'

'It is,' the man answered laconically, but with an unequivocal tone, showing that he was not intimidated. The man was dressed in a herring-bone jacket. He had the paper spread out on his lap, an umbrella by his side.

The fat man elbowed Ambrose again. He was getting hot, his head reddening as he smiled. His pink scalp showed a mottled colour under his thinning black hair. He put his head close to the man in the suit again. 'I could never make heads or tails of the *Irish Times*, do you know what I mean? The *Independent* or the *Herald* is my man. At least you understand what the hell they're on about.'

Ambrose watched the man in front tilt his head to the side. 'Do you mind?' was all the man said in a stiff tone. His grey hair had been perfectly parted with oil and a comb. It showed a certain distinction, the close shave and taut skin which had been well taken care of.

The fat man puffed his cheeks and drummed his fingers on the rail on the back of the seat. He looked around at the other people and rubbed his hands together. Ambrose wanted to get up, but stuck to his seat, his suitcase wedged between his knees.

The fat man took a small bottle of Paddy's from his coat and put it to his lips. His eyes squinted as he swallowed. 'Ah . . . ' He brought his sleeve across his lips when he was done. His lips and face took on a deep purple hue, the hidden veins beneath the skin coming to the surface. 'Nothin like it to get yous goin. Do yous want a sup?' He nudged Ambrose. 'Go on.'

'No thanks,' Ambrose waved his hand and tried to look at ease.

The fat man hunched himself forward, leaning over, almost touching the man's head in front with his big chin. The smell of whiskey filled the air. 'Does the *Irish Times* have a Sports section? There's a race in England I have my eye on.'

The man turned and handed a section of the paper to the fat man who said, 'That's grand altogether. Lets see here now.'

The fat man winked at Ambrose and mouthed, 'Posh,' loud enough for everyone to hear, nodding his head to the man who'd given him the paper. Then he drew his hand across his own hair, trying to flatten and smooth it. 'I say, ol' chap. There is a filly in the six at Camden I quite fancy.' He showed his small teeth when he smiled, blackened from neglect and drink. His breath was sweet with whiskey. 'Do yous have a match?' the fat man asked Ambrose.

'I don't smoke,' Ambrose answered without looking. Beads of condensation formed on the creamy-coloured roof studded with rivets.

The bus conductor came onto the upper deck, fumbling with coins in his leather bag. 'Fares, please.'

The fat man went on at Ambrose. 'Jasus almighty, you're a saint! Who the hell has a match? Do yous have one, boss?'

'Fares,' the conductor said, standing over the fat man.

'Right yous are, there. Do you have a match?' the fat man asked the conductor.

'I don't.' The conductor moved up the bus, planting each foot steadily, balancing and accounting for the motion of the bus.

'Who has a match?' the fat man said, turning around, waving his cigarette.

The man in front didn't react, just went on reading the paper silently.

The fat man took a match from a man across the way from him. He lit the match on the zipper of his anorak and held a cigarette. 'Lovely.' He held the smoke in his lungs. It came out in a blue whisper, his small mouth a perfect O, extinguishing the match in his hand. Even his nostrils smouldered as the smoke hung in the bus.

Ambrose opened the small window above him, the cold air blew the smoke about. A light drizzle drifted into the bus as it moved along. Ambrose shuddered and sucked in the cold air. He was on the verge of hitting the man, pushing him out of the seat and getting off, but he didn't dare move. He was leaving him alone for the most part anyway. Ambrose didn't want a scene. He wanted to get home to his mother before he was finished. He stayed put in his seat, gripping his bags.

The fat man directed his attention to the man in front of him. He directed his smoke off to the side of his mouth, letting it escape in small puffs. 'I don't know what this world is comin to. I'm for going up there and havin it out with them once and for all. Do you know? I don't know about yous, but that's the way I feel anyways. That's what I'm sayin. What does the *Irish Times* say? I bet they see it differently, but I'm only sayin what everybody thinks but is afraid to say. Well, I'm saying it now, so there!' His whole body quivered with the finality of his words. He looked around for support, his raised head looking up and down the bus.

Ambrose remained steadfast and said nothing. He strained to get the fresh air without appearing to move. Ambrose had always been conscious of the Englishness of Dublin on his trips in and out of the institution, the Victorian houses off by Stephen's Green, The Bank of Ireland and Dublin Castle, The Four Courts, all legacies of occupation. It was a city of the Empire and always would be. He could see there was a rift between those who aligned themselves with England and those with Dublin tenement accents, the city within the city, the tribe of Viking settlements, the hard-faced people up around Christ Church Cathedral. Ambrose knew nothing had ever been resolved in Dublin, let alone the North.

As the bus neared the city, some teenage boys got on, whistling and shouting, clamouring up onto the second floor of the double-decker. They carried Leeds United and Manchester United bags over their shoulder. They were heading off to a game somewhere in the city. They sat down in the front of the bus. They didn't wear overcoats, only black jackets with dingy white shirts. They all had cigarettes to their mouths.

Ambrose couldn't wait to get off the bus. The government could do nothing for the dissatisfaction in these places. The grip of an older world of horses and trading went on in its own clandestine manner. It was the country people like himself who had come up to Dublin to make its new middle class, not these men. These old Dubliners in their anoraks and corporation duffle coats were being sequestered in rundown areas. It would be a slow process, a dying out of one last generation in the city before they'd be moved out to the suburbs. All over the city, the grim process of letting areas fall into ruin had begun, the silent urban warfare. The great Georgian houses had begun a slow mitosis, the landlords renting by the room off the books. Ambrose made a sour face. It was happening all over the city. The bus passed another row of three-storey Georgian houses, the backs facing the road, curtainless and abject, rusting pipes hanging from the walls. The facades faced onto park greens. Ambrose had been through these types of parks before. They retained the absurd English symmetry of a bygone era, the arranged flower beds, the park benches, the oak trees placed fifteen feet apart. Monuments with splashing fountains gurgled impervious to change. The greens, conceived as man bettering nature, gave it shape and uniformity. In all things the hand of English genius should be apparent. Bushes that had once been shaped into swans or ducks were now overgrown, places for dogs to sniff, piss and defecate around, for gangs to gather and drink cider. The bus stopped and waited for a woman with three children to unfold her pram and get onto the bus. The conductor was down helping the woman. Ambrose rubbed the window with his hand. He could see the woman had come from one of the parks. The bus conductor struggled with the pram and then his money bag poured coins out onto the path. One of the woman's children started laughing and the conductor cursed. Ambrose closed his eyes.

The fat man gathered snot in his throat and spat it on the

floor, rubbing it with his big black boot. He took another sip from the whiskey, not bothering to screw back the top. The aroma mixed with the smell of smoke, giving a pub's intimacy to the bus. The fat man seemed lost for words, and then pulled on his cigarette, the red scab glowing. His tongue skimmed along his cheeks, turning the hot smoke. He touched the man in front with his cigarette. The ash crumbled and fell on the man's shoulder. 'Jasus, sorry about that.' The fat man cocked his head back as though ready to head-butt the man.

The man wiped away the ash and got up and moved two seats up.

'I said I was sorry, Jasus Christ.' He shook his head in disgust. Ambrose could see he was about to say something.

Ambrose thought about ringing the bell himself and leaving. He looked around to see if he could ally himself with the conductor, get him to ring the bell, but the conductor was downstairs. A small man in a tattered coat sat behind Ambrose eating a bag of Tayto cheese and onion. He looked at Ambrose and raised his thick eyebrows in acknowledgment, his unshaven silvery-haired face flecked with crumbs.

'I say lets go up North and sort this arseology out once and for all,' the fat man blurted out again. 'It's the only way to end this shite once and for all. Let's do what Michael Collins was afraid to do, go up and take back our country!'

The teenagers up front laughed to themselves. 'Fuck off!' one of them shouted. Another shouted, 'Let's see you read the Irish above the window there, Jacko.'

Ambrose began to shake. The effects of the morning were already at his nerves. He should have stayed in hospital. All these bodies around him. He felt eyes burning into his back.

The fat man jostled in his seat.

Ambrose shut his eyes and tried to shout as loud as he could in his mind.

The fat man ignored the teenagers. 'Nobody cares about this country at all,' he slurred. His head turned from side to side, the scruff of neck hair wet and plastered. He turned in his seat so his huge legs were in the aisle. He stomped his boots on the thin metal floor. 'You know what I say? I say fuck the lot of yous, yous dirty fuckin ol' ballocks! Such a shower of fuckin Beatles eejits.'

'Lay off,' one of the teenagers shouted back. 'You can't read a word of Irish.'

The fat man pointed his cigarette at the teenagers and then put the whiskey bottle to his chest and sang, 'Sinne Fianna Fáil Atá Fé gheall ag Érinn . . . '

'Keep going,' the teenagers jeered. 'You don't even know your National Anthem!'

The fat man stopped short, stuck. 'Irish has fuckin nothin to do with Dublin city! When did yous ever hear a person say an Irish word on the street?'

Ambrose's legs stiffened around his suitcase. The fat man's monstrous rump pressed close, the broad expanse of his back pivoting back and forth as he shouted and cursed. He forced Ambrose to move closer to the window until his shoulder touched his chin.

The fat man took another swig of whiskey. He looked around at Ambrose who caught his eye for a moment. 'And what are yous lookin at? Off on your fuckin holidays and the country about to go to war. Nobody gives a fuck about this country anymore, only me and the likes of me who know what was done to our people on these very streets that we're on right now! You're a culchey. Kerry, is it, or Cork? Cork, yeah, home of fuckin Michael Collins, that ballocks. He started all this business!' The fat man brought his swollen face close to Ambrose, two flecks of spit on either side of his mouth. 'Culcheys comin up to Dublin to work all week long, and then yous fuck off back down to the country for the weekend to spend your money. Dublin too dirty for yous? Good enough to make money in, but yous wouldn't want to live here!' The fat man put his hands on his thighs, pulling at his trousers. 'There's no consensus in this fuck hole of a place. Everybody does what the fuck they want! Partition in land, heart and body! That's what we have.'

'Give it up,' the bus conductor shouted from downstairs.

'Yes, give it up,' a man in an expensive pin-striped suit said quietly, rustling a newspaper, folding it into small squares which he read silently.

The fat man tapped Ambrose on the shoulder. 'Here's a good one for you, culchey! Are yous listening?

> *Are you from Cork, I am, are you?*
> *Do you ate spuds? I do, do you?*
> *How da you ate dem? Skin an' all.*
> *Wouldn't they choke ya? Not at all!*

Did you ever hear dat one before, culchey?'

Ambrose glared at him, his fist clenched. 'Could you say that in Irish?' he blurted.

The teenagers erupted in laughter and the fat man rolled his eyes.

'Shag off, culchey!' His swollen, yellowish fingers pressed against Ambrose. 'This is my town.'

'Dun do bheal, Jacko!' one of the teenagers shouted and winked. They were nearly obscured in their own layer of smoke, coughing and spitting out the window.

The fat man got out of his seat, almost falling with the sway of the bus. His bottle of whiskey turned in his pocket and spilled onto the floor. Ambrose flinched.

'Sit down!' an old woman cried. 'Have some decency, will you?'

The conductor ran up the stairs. 'You're off if I hear another word out of you, do you hear me?' His long thin fingers touched the fat man's back.

The fat man collapsed back into the seat beside Ambrose, almost breaking the seat with his tremendous weight. 'I hear yous,' he muttered. He took the bottle out of his pocket and looked at it in disgust. 'Listen, look! I just want to say this one thing here, now, all right. Let's get this straight. Speakin Irish has fuck all to do with anythin. I bet yous Molly Malone didn't know a word of Irish, and that's a fact!' The fat man shook his head. 'Not a word! I won't be jeered in my own town. I was bred and buttered here. My Dad fought in the streets of Dublin against the Black and Tans, so yous can fuck yourself, culcheys and sasanachs. Fucking Johnny-come-latelies! Fuck Leeds United and your Beatles, yous bastards!'

'Yeah, and fuck your Cross Channel Racing!' one of the teenagers shouted.

The fat man's nostril hairs hung out of his nose as he drew in deep breaths. 'This is my home, do yous hear me, culchey?' He said it in deep resignation, almost conscious of his own absurdity. His small eyes, rimmed in pink circles, welled. His face deflated, the chins spilling down onto the coarse black of his chest hair. 'In Dublin's fair city, where the girls are so

147

pretty, I first set my eyes on sweet Molly Malone . . . ' he started with renewed passion, wiping his face.

The conductor put his hand on the fat man's shoulder. 'Shut your face!'

The fat man let his head rest on a roll of his chin, and the tension eased as he hummed softly to himself.

The bus laboured along, the gears grinding, the diesel engine hammering. Loose panels vibrated. The windows were completely misted over. People moved their hands to pull through the skin of dampness. More people got on until people were standing in the aisle. The older women had on heavy coats, hats, handbags and leather gloves. Some women wore scarves, hair curled into pink rollers.

Ambrose looked up from his seat, the impassive faces heading into Dublin. A sullen tiredness fell. Even the fat man buried his head into the paper, took out a pen and circled a horse in a race. Every few seconds a branch tapped the bus as it moved along, a knotted finger pointing at Ambrose, leaves plastered against the damp glass. Ambrose tensed his face, looking at the walls outside plagued by moss and lichen, magpies in the gardens, the green patches of grass, the clothes on the line. A scarecrow with foil milk bottle tops for eyes glittered in a small vegetable patch. From the bus Ambrose could see into the secret bedrooms, a man smoking, looking out from lace curtains, another room with a solitary, exposed bulb hanging over a woman in a pink nightgown. Ambrose caught glimpses, just shades of someone else's life, lives he would never see again.

In these moments on the bus when he was left alone with his thoughts, he sometimes found a reprieve from the mania of his own existence. He could rest easy, coolly gazing out at things which could not impinge upon him.

The fat man beside Ambrose had nodded off to sleep, the pen still between his big fingers, a looping circle around a horse. Ambrose smiled faintly. His legs were numb. He felt the twinge of pins and needles in them, but he was relaxed. There would be no fight. The bus continued in its awful labour, wheezing and rattling. Anonymity had its luxury for a few moments. He was not Ambrose the lunatic, but just another passenger heading into Dublin. Ambrose came to the conclusion that the bus was one of the most dehumanizing, and thus liberating means of transportation he had ever been on.

At Aston Quay, Ambrose waited for another bus to Houston station. He breathed a sigh of relief, but his hands were shaking again now that he was exposed. Ambrose looked up at the sky. It was a cold, clear day. He could see his breath. The fat man was crossing the road, holding his arm up, stopping cars which beeped at him. Ambrose tensed his stomach. He needed to relieve himself but felt he should wait until he got to the train station.

All the talk going by him was about the North, pairs of men or women making a tisk tisk sound as they nodded to one another, the tap of umbrellas on the concrete. On a pole, Ambrose looked up the time schedule for the bus and then bit his lip, looking around him. Some of the shops had put up tricolour flags in windows showing support for the Catholics in the North. Ambrose stood with his luggage, pensive, eyeing his watch. He didn't want to miss the train. A wind had picked up, blowing rubbish around. He resolved he'd never come back to Dublin again. The job he had would do him if only he gave it a chance. Each time he went to the institution these past few times, they had him in for months. They had their own motivation. Medical histories charted over a long period of time, that was their game. There were no instant cures. Psychotherapy had moved decidedly into the realm of theory. They were beginning to shy away from prescribing as many drugs. He was their mouse in the maze. The age of group therapy was close at hand. He could see it now: Ambrose Feeney, charter member of 'Granny Bashers Anonymous'. Well, he wasn't going to let that happen. This madness of his could be controlled if he wanted to do it, and now he did. He wanted to rid himself of old hatred, forget the past.

A stern-faced man pushed by with a black band on his arm, signifying sympathy with the North. Ambrose drew back against the wall. He could sense their raucous nationalism, men without jobs, hard drinkers with nothing to look forward to. You might as well be a patriotic, unemployed, drunk man. It gave a certain dignity. These men around him had nothing, only a bastardized history. They had ancestors who had been through the great lockout and the 1916 rising, and what had they got in the new country?

The fat man only had his fags and his booze. There was a portion of the population who would never gain anything. Yet myth persisted precariously in drinking songs that held a decidedly sour nostalgia. The imminence of violence was always present. The fat man couldn't stop himself getting drunk, shouting, trying to articulate what had been done to him. And for all his frustration he could only shout about the North and freeing the Catholics. The government had it well measured. All governments provide one enemy to hate. But people played the English pools, and watched the Cross Channel Races, and the music was all English. Irish national-ism had a severe inferiority complex as far as Ambrose could see it.

Ambrose pulled his bags closer to his side. He kept looking for a bus, muttering to himself. Only oily puddles showed as buses pulled in and out. Ambrose checked his watch. Behind him, the Liffey stagnated at low tide giving off a rank stench of sewage. Ambrose looked down at the sludge of green mired mud littered with old prams, bicycles, bottles and old wheels. The sun was still only climbing into the sky.

A group of people gathered across the road. A man shouted into a bull horn. He had a sharp Northern accent. There was going to be a rally of some sort. Just hours ago the city had been asleep, Belfast and Derry as remote as something you'd see on the television, a distant war. Now people were gathering around, whistling and shouting about their brothers, wanting to start a war with England. Ambrose watched them gathering. Who the hell would they be fighting? Half of their relatives lived in London and Liverpool.

The North had become a political sideshow that could be dragged out when the economy was looking bad. Its instant rhetoric had its own charismatic aura. The Molly Malone, The Wolfe Tone, The Robert Emmett, were all talismans for a good song, the Guinness brewery getting rich on the sepia portraits of the men of 1916, sedate shots of unsmiling men, pictures of the GPO under siege, the faded nostalgic images caught in time, promoting the sense that all Ireland's troubles lay in it being a divided nation.

In a matter of minutes, the sky darkened, and it rained. A blue sky opened, and then it poured again in typical Dublin fashion. The sun hung in the cold air. Ambrose looked up at the sky. A light sleet drifted overhead, falling to the ground in muted splats, the opaque droplets melting on the road. People moved quickly, some with umbrellas up, the red knotted fists braving the stinging cold. Others almost ran with their hands deep in their coats, collars turned up, resigned to the weather. The cool sun poured through the sky despite the sleet. Ambrose stood under the bus shelter and moved to keep warm. He stomped his foot, holding back the urine in his bladder, the tincture of pain running to the tip of his penis. He moved his hands inside his trousers.

A middle-aged woman in a scarf with the imprint of fruit came under the shelter with her two boys linked together, dressed identically in blue blazers and grey shorts. They each carried a plastic prayer book and had little white sashes on their lapels. Their thin legs had bluish circles from the cold sleet which had turned to rain and now stopped. The mother smiled to an old lady whose legs ended in swollen ankles and oversized shoes. 'Bitter weather,' the mother said.

Ambrose looked out at the sky. There was the possibility of another shower off out by Howth head. The two boys grinned at one another. Their hair was stuck to their heads. They were both counting money. Their father, a man in a shiny tuxedo jacket with a trimming of velvet came bustling across the road with a paper bag under his arm. He had two six-packs of stout. 'We're all set then,' he smiled to his wife. 'So, who's winnin,' he grinned to his two boys.

'They all give us the same, Dad. You know that.'

The mother slapped one of the boys on the shoulder. 'Put that money away. It's not right to be counting money. You made your communion, not opened a business.'

The father had big oyster eyes from too many drinks at the relatives' houses already. He rubbed his large nose with his hand. 'That's right. Remember, all that money is goin into your post office books, so don't get too attached to it.'

'Yeah, we know what that means,' one of the boys groaned.

Ambrose looked away and tried to see if the bus was coming. He needed to take his medicine. From his pocket he took out a bottle of medicine and swallowed two tablets. The chalky taste hung on his throat. He gathered spit and moved his tongue around in his mouth.

'What's that, Dad?' one of the boys said.

Ambrose and the rest of them stared over at two old men who started playing a bodhrán and a whistle outside a pub. They were hunched over their instruments. Two pints of porter stood sentry in the coldness. A dirge-like effect rose in the blustery air. A crowd began to gather, men coming out from the pubs, drinks raised, the smoke of their breath rising into the air. Big men with monstrous porter bellies stood sternly on squat legs, nodding to one another. The sky, now clear, made everything seem slightly unnatural and bright, the street incandescent as the sun hit the dripping beads of rain running off the buildings.

'Do they want to go over and have a look?' the father said.

'We're going to my mother's. Stay put,' his wife answered stiffly. 'I don't want you near a pub.'

The father made a face at the two boys and they laughed. His wife turned and took his arm. 'Give it over, Tommy.' She smiled and drew herself close to her husband's arm and locked her body to his. 'We're not going over there, all right, Tommy?'

The father kissed her forehead. 'This is your day, don't worry yourself.'

Finally a bus pulled in. It took over half an hour to get

down to the station. The bus was diverted from the quays. A band of men were pushing their way to the Four Courts, demanding action be taken. Ambrose watched the throngs milling around. He opened the window, heard the shouting and cursing, men jostling one another. They were all unwashed, hair greasy and long, dressed in cheap suits with trousers too short for them. A crowd of hippies in flared trousers and platform shoes had also gathered. They carried flowers and sheets with 'Give Peace a Chance' sprayed in hot pink.

Filthy children stood in the narrow streets, off to the side, the small red brick houses trailing off into lanes hung with clothes. The children held plastic dolls and checkered black and white footballs.

When Ambrose reached the station, he looked back down the quays, seeing the skeletal arch of the ha'penny bridge spanning the Liffey, smoke rising from all the hidden houses. A serene silence prevailed. Ambrose was conscious of the smell of the Guinness brewery churning vats of dark liquid behind its great walls.

Ambrose boarded the midday train to Limerick, found a toilet and drained himself. His body was sapped of energy. He found an empty seat, curled up and slept until he reached Limerick three hours later.

A neighbour who worked at the station spotted Ambrose when he arrived and took him to his car. 'You're doing OK are you?' the neighbour said, eyeing Ambrose suspiciously.

'Are you sure it's no bother, Mr Norris?' Ambrose said.

Mr Norris checked his watch in the breast pocket of his station master's uniform and winked. His greying eyebrows came together when he smiled. 'Nothing until the half two from Limerick junction. I'll take you down.'

Ambrose nodded and shuffled along, his body lost in his coat, his hair dishevelled from sleep. Sounds echoed in the station, pigeons cooing overhead in the rafters, the place splattered with droppings.

Mr Norris spat once they came out of the station. 'Jasus, it's cold. Was it cold in Dublin?' His breath turned into a thick cloud as he breathed.

'It was cold enough,' Ambrose answered. He felt a sudden faintness and leaned on Mr Norris's shoulder.

Mr Norris nearly buckled under Ambrose's weight. 'Are you all right?' Mr Norris struggled to help Ambrose sit down on the stone steps outside the station. The stone was glazed in a thin frost.

'I just needed . . . The fresh air is . . . ' Ambrose gasped for breath.

Mr Norris loosened Ambrose's tie. 'I'll call for a doctor,' Mr Norris went on, fumbling with the thick knot of Ambrose's tie.

Ambrose's face turned a hot pink. He looked up at Mr Norris. 'I'm grand, really.'

Mr Norris's small face showed a child's perplexity when he was confronted by something he could not fathom. 'Someone should have been up to meet you,' he said severely. 'It's a disgrace.'

Finally, Ambrose and Mr Norris set off. They drove along the road, Mr Norris ran his fingers over the steering wheel, eyeing Ambrose. He said tentatively, 'So do you think it's going to blow over up there? That's only the impression I have, and I know nothing of what goes on up North, only I'm thinking it would be hard to do nothing and not look like an eejit at this stage of the game. We should send up the Army, if only to save face at this stage.'

'There was a march up in Dublin,' Ambrose managed to say.

'I heard about it on the radio. God, you'd think it was another country they were talking about sometimes, like you know what I'm saying? It's not that you wouldn't feel sorry for them up there, but . . . ' Mr Norris beeped his horn and slowly pulled out, passing a boy riding bareback on a horse. The horse moved slowly, a chestnut mare with a string of twine tied around the pale brownish nostrils. The horse flicked its tail, dropping dark green balls of manure.

'Where was I . . . Yeah . . . God almighty, I hate it when the horses leave a mess like that. Get out of it, young fella. Go on.' Mr Norris leaned out of his window, his small bottom raised off the seat.

Mr Norris drew his head in again. He saw Ambrose shivering. 'The heat's coming now.' He put his hand over the vent. 'There, it's getting warm.' He wiggled his nose. 'Can you smell that shite still?'

Ambrose nodded solemnly.

Mr Norris lit a cigarette with the red coil of the cigarette lighter. He was about to give one to Ambrose. 'You still don't . . . ' He nodded to the cigarette.

'No, thank you all the same, I won't.'

As the car moved along the narrow road, Ambrose looked at the fresh IRA graffiti all over the walls, murals of Sarsfield and NO SURRENDER! sprayed everywhere.

'Look at that for God's sake,' Mr Norris hissed in disgust. 'The IRA and Sarsfield are as different as night and day. Honest to God, the stupidity of these old eejits when they get going. I'm as nationalistic as the next man, but sure what can we do down here? We only manage barely. Amn't I right? Sure my Frank is over in England and married. Can you imagine the carry-on he has to go through all the time?'

The narrow street intersected lanes that dated back beyond the famine. Limerick's labyrinth of shadows and doorways, the musty smell of sawdust sprinkled outside doorways, the city within the city, the lanes dipping down slants where the water rushed during heavy downpours. Things were bartered for other things in the lanes. There were people in there who had not come out in years, occupying the domains of small pubs and little shops tucked into the sides of walls. They had no interest in coming out into the city. Ambrose liked the feeling of enclosure, the murky window fronts hiding those inside, commerce carried on in secrecy, the hidden account books fixed so the tax man couldn't understand them. Ambrose felt the hint of movement in the shadows of the place. There were others like him. Displacement was sequestered in these narrow passages. He didn't need an institution to hide from the world.

'Jack Lynch says that Ireland is not going to stand idly by and let its people be killed. If they're not fighting words, I don't know what are, but I'll tell you, I don't know if it wouldn't be best to just let this thing die down for now at least until the two governments can sit down together and come to some arrangement. I think that's the way it should go. Now that's just me talking, but I think I know what I'm on about. At the station, the union and management never discuss anything in the heat of an argument. It's easy to say something, but harder to take it back. Amn't I right? I know I'm right, right?'

'Right,' Ambrose answered.

Mr Norris bunched himself over the steering wheel, the cigarette balanced to the side of his thin lips which strained toward the partially open window. 'Jesus, this is unnaturally cold. I heard we're in for another ice age. That's what I read in the paper. This scientist says the North Pole will get hot and we'll get cold. Can you beat that now, Ambrose?'

Proto-Limerick types, small little men with pinched weasel faces and small teeth, hands behind their backs, and others big and cumbersome, heavy drinkers moved around chatting with one another, tipping their caps on their heads, saluting the women in slippers and aprons with scarves on their heads, coming and going from shops. Ambrose saw a woman prodding a cabbage, checking its freshness. A small little man in a jumper talked to the woman inspecting his vegetables.

Ambrose guessed they had to be talking about the weather. It was a safe subject.

Fraternity had its sharp side, as Ambrose well knew. The men got work done despite themselves. It was a constant effort to appear as though you had nothing to do, but they pulled it off.

Each return to Limerick made the place seem more antiquated. The three months in Dublin had been like an eternity. The old walls of the city were in desperate shape. They would have called Limerick a case study in pervasive and contented apathy up in the institution, a semi-conscious fatalism lived with a smile.

Ambrose knew them for what they were worth, though. He'd been away, but that had given him time to put things into perspective, to understand at least some of the madness. To tell the truth, the people in the city didn't tell the truth, the entire population conspirators even against themselves. The car came to a stop at a light. Ambrose looked over at a woman holding up a turnip, almost weighing it in her freckled hand. She was buying the last of the day's vegetables for the next day's dinner, trying to get a few pence off the turnip. She had an empty bag on her other thick arm.

Ambrose looked at her, a woman who told only what suited her, building part of the indomitable character of Limerick women, always fortifying herself with this and that story. Ambrose remembered the story of an aunt of his who'd been diagnosed with cancer and told she had six months to live. She returned home and said she was too busy for cancer. She had dinner to get for her husband and children and dismissed the whole thing. She was still living to this day. The same kind of story circulated around the stalls among the women. They had all overcome some hardship, and it was up to yourself not to let things happen to you. Of course, there were no stories of his other aunt who had wasted away for two years in Barrington's hospital. No, there was no place for that enigma. It was better to let it go unsaid. It was the will of God. There was a selectivity in the stories that people told. Their naïveté was not stupidity. For some people, intelligence was knowing the right questions to ask, but here negation was the game, knowing the right questions not to ask.

Mr Norris put in the clutch and the car pulled away from the lights. Ambrose could see the woman putting the turnip into her bag, the small grocer taking the money in his open palm. Another small battle had ended in Limerick, dinner would be served for one more day.

It was good to have an eejit like Norris roaming around the town, looking for an excuse to leave his job for a while. The crowds were now pouring into the streets. It pleased Ambrose, allowed him to recatalogue his life in an easy manner. The providence of routine had its numbing effect. The provincialism he'd loved as a boy still prevailed. He could hide away in this city for the rest of his life. He would never leave his home again, never let himself go back to Dublin. The three months he'd spent in the institution in Dublin would be his last. There was peace here in Limerick with his mother and father. This was where he was born, and where he'd die in his own self-conscious anguish and be just like all the rest of them. He'd reached the point where he knew he would do nothing in this world of any significance. Now the challenge was to ally himself with mediocrity, which, no matter how easy it looked, took a certain talent. But he was willing to learn, to start again with no expectations.

Mr Norris had been talking away and nudged Ambrose. 'You're OK, are you?'

Ambrose smiled but said nothing. He could see Mr Norris had been on for a big discussion on the situation up in the North. But Ambrose didn't feel like conceding these brief moments of re-experiencing the city. He continued to look silently out the small windshield at the people moving around, the same old characters as always. The place would never reach that point where a mass of people could preserve their own anonymity while dealing with one another. Limerick was too small. Everyone knew everyone else. He'd been told up at the hospital that rats acted differently when they reached a certain ratio of rats to space, as though some other consciousness set in. From an economic standpoint, they were all one step above hunters and gatherers, coming to market, bartering and buying bits of this and that, dealing in live animals killed on the spot. Limerick was the slaughter capital of Ireland, every word and action driven by a solid meal of animal meat. Limerick: the meat and potatoes dynasty of the world. In Limerick you could not buy something from someone without knowing that person somewhat, and therefore without begrudgingly thinking, 'That fucker already has a grand house, and look at me!' This accounted for the tenuous fraternity, the strangling chatter, handshakes holding you in place, the battles going on all over the place. Ambrose rubbed his face and felt the strain of exhaustion as well as the exhilaration of understanding.

Here, everyone took things personally. Not enough rat consciousness per square mile yet. Ambrose, sitting in the small confines of the car, looked around and smiled for the first time in ages. He was home.

'What are you laughing at?' Mr Norris said, pulling on his cigarette. 'Are you sure you're all right? There's not much to laugh about in this world today. When you see the television . . . '

Ambrose nodded but did not listen. He kept staring out the window, the car snaking its way past a horse-drawn flatbed loaded with coal. The echo of metal hooves against the concrete brought peace to Ambrose. And then a man about his father's age slipped in through a gap between two cars, his handlebars balanced with two plastic bags of something, and Ambrose smiled to himself again. All the ways man was trying to define life, just so he could live it. Ambrose eased his legs, letting them stretch in the car filled with sweet wrappers and discarded cigarette boxes. Here it was, this enigma, life, the thing he couldn't cope with, going on in Limerick, acted out by seasoned veterans, the old and the young, the old man on the bicycle, a small boy selling the newspaper with a sing-song Limerick accent on a corner, his neighbour driving his car, playing the system, knowing when the train came in. They had all learned to live in Limerick. Like no other country on the face of the earth. Other countries were known for their philosophers. The intent of a society was laid down in philosophical ideals going back to Greeks and Romans. But when the Romans arrived at Hadrian's Wall, they looked at one another and said, 'Let's stop here. I don't like the look of this lot.' They never got here, so off in places like Limerick things remained unchanged. Of course there was a rudimentary philosophy tacked on to character, the Irish humour, their turn of phrase, but it wasn't pure philosophy. It was, as Ambrose had said all those years ago, 'Pure animal.'

Mr Norris pulled over and picked up another neighbour

Ambrose recognized, but couldn't name. 'I know you,' was all the man said when he saw Ambrose, his big face smiling. The two men started into talk about the North right away. Ambrose could smell the drink on the man's breath. 'Are you on for a pint?' the neighbour said, pudgy-faced, teeth missing in his head. Mr Norris flipped open his watch, then looked into his rearview mirror and winked. 'Maybe just the one.'

'Jasus, its bitter cold.'

Mr Norris agreed. 'I was just saying that I heard that we're heading for another ice age . . . '

'Isn't that all we need,' the neighbour concurred in disgust, rubbing his hands together the way Ambrose did sometimes when his nerves were at him. The two men went into a series of monologues.

Ambrose listened to none of it and left the car without saying anything.

'Take care of yourself, Ambrose,' Mr Norris called out, still smoking away in the front of the car. Ambrose turned and nodded as the car bucked out into the road, turning in a U and heading off toward the town. Ambrose tried to settle his nerves, feeling the first jitters in his stomach.

He took a deep breath, turned and walked to his house.

Tom answered the door, and the look he gave betrayed just how bad Ambrose looked. 'What are you doing here?' His brother had his foot wedged in the door as though he wasn't going to let Ambrose in.

Ambrose shrugged his shoulders and pushed his way into the hallway. 'That's some kind of homecoming,' he said stiffly. He hadn't seen Tom in over six months.

Tom bit his lip, almost faltering with the smell of Ambrose's breath. He put his hand to his face, flushed with a sudden embarrassment. 'How did you get here? Jesus Christ.' Tom stood obstinately in the hallway, blocking the sitting room door. He spoke in a strained whisper. 'I thought the hospital said you couldn't come out for a few weeks. That's what they told me this morning.' His thin body stayed rigid as he spoke.

'That was just a misunderstanding.' Ambrose's watery eyes darted around the old place, the two statues on the sideboard with the withered petals at their feet. His body shook with their proximity, the cold alabaster porcelain sheen. 'He's in there, is he?' Ambrose swallowed, looking at the sitting room door. He felt himself panting. His heart raced in his chest.

'We didn't expect you,' Tom whispered. 'There's too many

165

people in there. You can't just walk in like that. The children and everything.' Mumbling came from behind the door. The door opened an inch. An eye peaked out and then the door started to close again. 'Jesus Christ . . . ' someone muttered. 'It's Ambrose.'

Tom averted his eyes. The door shut, the warm air rushing into the hall.

'I've come home to be with him,' Ambrose said softly. 'I've come home, Tom. It's going to be different from now on.' His head nodded as he spoke. 'I'm a changed man, and I'm giving you my word, as God is my witness, that it's all over now . . . ' Ambrose stopped and wiped his face with his hand.

Tom stood in the hallway, a taller version of Ambrose with a balding head, scant hair plastered to the side, his body lean in his suit. He just missed looking respectable, something about the suit, the sleeves too short, the trousers pinched at the crotch, and an overall crumpled look about it. He stood his ground though, a resignation of weariness apparent on his long face. 'That's good to hear, Ambrose.' Tom wet his lips, his thin tongue coming out of his mouth. 'I think it would be better to wait before you go in. There's no hurry now that you're here.'

Ambrose put his hands into his pockets and bent his head. His body jerked under his long coat. 'If you think it's best,' he said. 'I don't want any more trouble, Tom. That's all in the past, right, Tom?'

'That's good to hear . . . because . . . ' Tom's forehead wrinkled as he searched for something to say but he could think of nothing.

Ambrose felt the apathetic fatalism in Tom's face. Tom couldn't even bring himself to speak to him. It was hard that two brothers should have drifted so far apart. Ambrose looked at the two statues and touched the foot of the Virgin Mary. 'On our Blessed Mother's heart, I swear it's all over now, Tom.' His hand ran over the cold alabaster foot, his finger tracing its way over the head of the serpent Mary crushed beneath her foot.

Ambrose knew there was no point in starting a row at this stage of the game with Tom, two brothers meeting after a time apart, seeing the age creeping on one another. The vague affinity of shared genes made them stare a moment too long at one another. It was a resignation borne out of mutual lethargy. What was the point in renewing anything, of trying to pretend that being brothers meant anything anymore? Tom closed his eyes and rubbed his face with his hands. 'I have to go in to them.'

Ambrose opened his mouth, and his face relaxed, showing that he did not want trouble and he said, 'I'll have a cup of tea if it's no trouble.' Then he turned toward the stairs. 'You'll be leaving soon, I suppose?'

Tom's thin lips relaxed. 'I'll bring up the tea.' Tom stood in the middle of the hallway, his head tilted back as Ambrose ascended the stairs.

Ambrose felt the loss of power in his legs. He strained his head like a tortoise, using the banister to support himself, his feet scanning each step tentatively, his boot finding each step with a soft thud. The effects of the shock treatment and the pills had slowed him considerably.

The landing held a pocket of cold air, a dim darkness with each bedroom off to the side. Ambrose remembered the time his father had hit him in the face right where he stood. He almost saw him there. Dust swirled in the half-light. The toilet made a gurgling noise as usual. Ambrose's lungs ached with the coldness. A shudder passed through him.

Ambrose opened his bedroom door. It was the same as he'd left it, the sour odour of his stale clothes and bed sheets, something he smelt with memory, not his nostrils, a debilitating flow of water coming to his eyes. He tasted his tears. He was home.

The light fell on the far wall, the wallpaper peeled and faded from years of mildew. It smelled vaguely of formaldehyde, or of the hospital up in Dublin. Ambrose looked at the wardrobe. His government uniforms were wrapped in paper from the cleaners as though he'd not been away at a mental institution at all. The bed was up against the wall, the squat dresser with the broken mirror. How many times had he looked at his fractured image in its broken glass through the years? His shaving items were there along with a bottle of holy water. A layer of dust had settled during the three-month absence. The room of a lunatic. Everything felt like it could explode.

He took a deep breath and squeezed the tension in his temples. It was better to have them gone before seeing his father downstairs. He went to the window and stared down into the neighbour's garden, the long rectangle of perfect order, the shed at the end for the tools, the vegetable patch laced in mesh for the winter, and then the margin of perfect green garden with the flower beds. Everything was the same. He felt the slow contentment, the cataloguing of what he knew and expected from life, the familiar backdrop of thirty-odd years of living in the same house, looking out at the same back garden. His mind ran over the past and eased him.

He looked down at his own back garden, less uniform, the

cement shed with the crescent wall for the pigs. The grass had been churned into mud. Beside the clothes-line, a trail had been worn, his father's coming and going to the coal bunker, filling it to capacity through the years. The neighbours had really let them away with murder. Even Ambrose had to admit that much. Such civilized city people burdened with the likes of his country-bred father. Nobody else raised pigs in the city now.

Ambrose saw Mr Danaher coming out to the clothes-line and watched him surveying his garden. He had that look of supreme satisfaction, a man turning old with a good family behind him. Ambrose put his head against the glass and breathed, making the glass mist. He smelt the damp mildew in the old putty, the oily paint clotted in drips, hairs and flies trapped. The window was painted shut. Ambrose pressed the frame with the palm of his hand until the paint skin tore away.

Mr Danaher started to hang up the clothes. Ambrose watched him and then looked for a pig to emerge from the shed. In the past he used to open the window and throw out bits of toast or a few sweets for the pigs. He had liked seeing them running around. It detracted from the boredom sometimes.

No pig came out of the shed. Ambrose opened the window and made a clicking sound and felt the cold air stream in. Mr Danaher turned and saluted Ambrose. 'You're back,' he said.

Ambrose smiled.

'How's your father?'

The window rattled. 'Grand,' Ambrose answered and then looked at the shed again. There was none of the usual smell of animal waste. 'Hey, pigs!' Ambrose called out. But they didn't come.

'The pigs are gone,' Mr Danaher said, putting down his load of clothes. The wind made the hanging clothes dance on the line beside him. Mr Danaher was dressed in a creamy-coloured Aran island jumper that one of his children must have brought back from holidays. He'd taken to this sort of luxury. The Danahers were a close family, obliging and friendly. 'Your brother had some men come and take them away. It was last Wednesday, I think.'

Ambrose said nothing and turned to the bed. He took off his shoes. His feet were killing him. He set himself down onto the bed, still in his long coat, pulled the covers over his body and tried to sleep. His eyes fluttered under the lids, but he couldn't sleep. Things were different when they should have been the same. He expected to hear the grunt of the pigs down below. His ears kept listening for the sound, even though Mr Danaher had said they were gone. The great parochialism of his life had centred around the unchanging spectacle of his own house, the constant vigil of his mother at the fire, his father coming and going. All this had remained for so long, even when he was away at the lighthouse and up in the institution. At least he could set his mind at ease, and think that there was something recurring over and over again at his house. It was the satisfaction children got from stories told the same way over and over again.

Ambrose listened to the mutter of voices down in the sitting room. He was right over everybody. He got out of bed and put his ear to the floor and tried to listen and then heard Tom coming up the stairs and jumped back into the bed and curled up.

Tom came in with the mug of tea on a tray and set it down

on the carpet.

Ambrose opened his eyes and followed his brother's retreat, the shadow falling across the bed. 'Wait,' he whispered and turned his head. Only Ambrose's eyes were visible, moving slowly in their sockets. The small window cast a solid corridor of light on his brother.

Tom stood at the end of the bed dressed in his ill-fitting suit. He looked like a man who had returned from a funeral.

'What happened to him?' Ambrose whispered.

Tom stood motionless, his eyes like beads. He said nothing for a moment and then said, 'They found him out on the main road in a ditch with his bicycle. He was gone two days before . . . ' He left it at that.

Ambrose closed his eyes as though he were about to fall asleep and then opened them again, breathing deeply. A foot emerged from under the covers. Ambrose tried to pull himself up.

Tom hesitated and then drew the curtains. The place turned semi-dark. 'You should rest.'

The springs on the bed creaked as Ambrose shifted his weight. 'And then what happened?'

Tom stopped in the sullen light, his balding head shining. The smell of Ambrose's own body odour filled the room, the murkiness of evening settling. Tom opened the window, inhaling the cold like a man who had come up for air from the depths. 'He had a stroke,' Tom said softly, turning around.

'I need a glass of water for my tablets,' Ambrose said.

Tom went into the bathroom and came back and set down a glass of water beside the tea. Their eyes met inches from one another, the embarrassment of their failings apparent to both of them. Tom looked away. Ambrose saw the jaded look in his brother's eyes, the sexless man with seven children. His

171

brother had no room left for compassion at this stage. Ambrose wished he'd just leave.

There was shouting out on the street. Tom went to the window and peered out beyond the garden to a narrow road. 'We're going to have to get a move on if we want to get back to Galway.'

Ambrose had his eyes shut. 'What happened to the pigs?'

'There might be a war out of this yet. The place is up in arms.' Tom bit his lower lip, letting the curtain fall. Tom left the room and closed the door with a soft click and Ambrose waited until he heard Tom's voice down in the sitting room. He took the cup in the gloomy darkness, the greying aura of falling light outside trickling in through the slits in the curtain. Distant shouting filtered into the room. The tea had sugar in it, and Ambrose made a face and set it down beside the bed.

Ambrose went downstairs in his bare feet, so as not to make any noise, and went into the kitchen for a cup of tea. He turned on the cooker and sat down. The rings smoked, burning off old milk stains. The concrete floor was freezing as always. Ambrose wiggled his toes, looking around him. The kitchen had been his father's quarters through the years, the cold stony walls painted in glossy yellow, the solitary table sheeted with a thin film of plastic slashed by the bread knife, from the meals his father ate alone in the kitchen late at night. There had been a peace to his father's solitary vigils. He remembered listening to the scrape of the chair on the concrete telling him his father was about. Ambrose used to go down sometimes when he couldn't sleep. If his father was in good humour, he'd warm some milk for Ambrose, or tell him a story. Ambrose felt a smile on his lips. He'd expected to see his father here, despite the sickness. This was where his father had always sat in his long coat, drinking plain tea and eating bread, or settling down to a feed from the sweep-the-floor soup, or repairing a bicycle in the cold. To have moved from room to room would have suggested a change of mood, something to which his father had never been prone.

Tom stood with one hand in his pocket and a drink in the other. His body blotted the light from the hallway. 'You're up again?' he said laconically, his eyebrows raised in a vexed cross.

'Where are the pigs?' Ambrose asked.

'There are no pigs now.' Tom shook his head. His forehead and ears had turned a soft purple from the drink. 'We don't have time for this.' His eyes wandered in his head and then found their focus. 'You're not well enough to be out of the hospital. I think you should get back on the train tonight.' Tom nodded to his own suggestion.

Ambrose nodded in the same rhythmic manner. They were like two agitated machines. 'Maybe I will.' Ambrose stood up and went to the cooker and took the kettle off the boil. 'I don't take sugar,' he said, pouring water into a metal teapot. Ambrose could feel the presence of the people on the other side of the wall, inches from him. He felt like giving the wall a good kick and sorting them out. They were whispering to themselves, about him of course. 'If the others left, could I see him with you?' Ambrose said, turning and facing Tom. The spout of the kettle sent up a thin mist of steam beside Ambrose. 'I'm not going anywhere until I see him.' He settled the kettle down again and looked at Tom.

'What do you want me to do?'

'I want to see him, Tom. I don't want to see him alone, please.'

Tom closed the door and left. Ambrose got down on his knees and peered through the keyhole, seeing the procession of relatives leaving through the front door. Then he sat down again and put the mug of tea to his mouth, smiling. He still had some control in his own house. He felt like his father for a moment and tried to think of something his father might have said.

Ambrose heard them out in the hall. The warmth of the mug cradled in his palms and a slice of soda bread seemed all he could ever want in the world. Ambrose went to take a sip of the tea and became conscious that he was trembling again.

Tom came back in and opened the door. 'I have very little time,' he said. 'We have to get to Galway.' He still held the drink in his hand. Straight whiskey, Ambrose smelt its sweetness in Tom's pores. He'd been drinking all day, no doubt, but it was only showing now. On nights like this, when the darkness had begun to settle and the rain was falling, what if his brother went out onto the Galway road and fell asleep at the wheel with the children and a wife in the car with him? Was he the only one who found it peculiar for a father to take the lives of his wife and children into his hands every time he drove his car?

Ambrose put his tea down, put his hands on his lap and pushed himself up. His feet tingled when he put pressure on them.

Tom walked into the room, his shoulders sloped forward.

Ambrose steadied himself and went into the room. His father was sitting beside the blazing fire, a skeleton of his former self, dressed in a V-neck jumper and a white shirt with a heavy-knotted tie. His upturned eyes acknowledged

Ambrose with a soft blink.

Ambrose tensed his legs, the surge of blood flowing to his face. 'Dad,' he whispered.

Three war medals were pinned to his father's jumper beside his Sacred Heart Pledge pin. Even the old IRA scroll that had been up in his father's room was now placed behind his father as he sat in the chair. He seemed the main feature in a shrine.

'Dad . . . It's me, Ambrose,' Ambrose whispered, staring at the calcified image of him. He took his father's hand in his own, stroking the bony wrist. Ambrose rubbed his father's hand frantically like a child patting a small creature. His father let the hand be taken, smiled faintly, and licked his lips. His face was all bone. He seemed on the verge of saying something but only moved his thumb over Ambrose's hand. His father had always possessed an economy of expression. Now each movement was subordinate to a deathly weakness.

'Easy now, Ambrose. He's tired,' Tom said. 'He's had a long day.'

Ambrose tried to fight the tears, clamping his teeth and forcing his face into a grimace. His father felt very warm, the effect of the roasting fire. Even his clothes had a smoky hotness. Ambrose still held the hand. 'I'm here to mind you, Dad,' Ambrose whispered. The tears ran down his neck and disappeared beneath his shirt.

The door to the sitting room opened and Ambrose's mother stood there, looking in at Ambrose. She touched Ambrose before he could rise, whispering, 'Are you feeling all right, son?'

Ambrose stood up.

'You've been saying your prayers, Ambrose, I hope.'

Ambrose nodded his head. 'Yes, Mam.' A sudden vacuity

of emotion filled him, a surge of blackness, the rush of blood and drugs racing through his body. The palpable smell of baby powder from her set him off. He forgot his father for a moment. There she was, standing before him again, the source of all his misery, the stories he'd told about her, what he wanted to do to her, the names he had for her, and of course, she'd heard about it from the doctors, but here she stood, if not impervious, then sure in some faith that she would survive all this, her husband's dying and her son's mental illness.

'We all need prayer in this world.' She spoke softly, her eyes sunk into a nest of wrinkles. Tom took her by the elbow gently and led her to a seat.

Ambrose looked down at her swollen ankles, her knotted feet pinched into her black shoes. She seemed to walk on tip-toes. She let herself collapse into the sagging chair and put her thick hands together over her handbag. 'He fell off his bicycle,' she said breathlessly. She pointed toward the road.

Ambrose looked at the handbag in her lap. He knew she'd been giving out his money to her grandchildren.

Ambrose looked at his father who had his eyes on his wife.

Ambrose sat down at the table. The cups began to jitter on the saucers. The curtain behind him fluttered in the cold night air. 'I'm on new tablets,' Ambrose said, for lack of anything else to say. He reached into his pocket and took out a brown bottle and shook it. 'There'll be no more trouble from me. It was all a chemical imbalance . . . ' He faltered and stopped, putting a hand to his forehead. Jesus, why wouldn't Tom say something?

Tom stood awkwardly near his mother looking at Ambrose. He eyed the bottle of whiskey on the table, but left it alone, swilling the remains of the whiskey in his glass.

Ambrose scratched himself behind the head and puffed his cheeks in a distracted way. He picked at something in his teeth with his finger. He was conscious of his naked feet for the first time. It added to the affliction of his illness, an abject primitivism, showing his hairy toes to all before him. 'I'm better!' he blurted out. 'The tablets.' He shook the bottle.

'Has Tom said anything to you?' his mother asked. She touched Tom's trouser leg and moved away from the fire. His father made a moaning sound.

Ambrose shook his head. His mother was a right specimen, dressed up and washed, her hair brushed out, a nest of a hat on her head with artificial fruit and a brooch at her neck and a handbag in her hands. One generation removed from shawls, but the atavistic hunch of her shoulders remained despite her efforts to look like a posh Protestant. Ambrose gave her one of his patent grave stares. She looked away, her mouth moving with the cud of a prayer. 'You ol' whore,' he said to himself, working his teeth away at the nail on his small finger, sucking spit. He could see she'd anticipated this day for years. The run-down mechanism in her husband's chest was bound to give out eventually, feeds of pig slop and bread, always sacrificing for his children, eating the fatty rind. His mother saw him staring at her and made a slight gesture, muttering some indiscernible prayer. Ambrose could see that the grand matriarch was coming into her reign. The religiosity that had loomed for so many years could now settle without anybody passing comment. She would have her life back again, dressed up and ready to leave this house for ever if she wanted. She'd lived in the shadow of men all her life, but now she would inherit what they left behind. The blight of those years in the company of a man she hated were drawing to a close. Such smug satisfaction set against his own dissatisfaction, the margin of six feet separating them.

'You poxy bitch,' Ambrose whispered unconsciously, and then said it again, only conscious of it now. That was what he'd taken to calling her at the hospital, the greatest scrounge of a money-grabbing ol' whore that he'd ever had the misfortune to know. He swallowed and licked his lips, turning his head away.

Ambrose's mother looked at Tom.

'We think he needs attention in a home,' Tom finally said, his hands laced together before him. 'He has medical needs which nobody here can give him.' He spoke without conviction. He stepped forward and took the bottle of whiskey and topped up his glass and drank.

Ambrose looked up. 'No!' He banged the table with his fists. 'I'll take care of him. I've been here all these years, haven't I?'

His mother whispered something to Tom. She had a pronounced hobble now when it suited her. Ambrose was well aware of her antics, fit as a fiddle one minute, and feigning ill health the next. She'd done that for years, getting her own way despite everyone.

'I think it would be best if you went up to Dublin for the time being, until things get settled here,' Tom managed to say. He put his arms up in a helpless gesture, his suit sleeves inching up his arms, the white sleeves of his shirt showing with their fake gold cufflinks. 'You can do nothing here at this stage.'

'Wouldn't you be better away from this sort of thing?' Ambrose's mother chimed in, holding Tom for support. 'If you're on good tablets, why don't you give them a chance to work. You have to take care of yourself, Ambrose.'

'I've lived here all my life.' Ambrose said defiantly.

'Only a professional can take care of him now,' Tom persisted, the sullen melancholy of a man in need of more drink. He looked at his watch and then at his mother. He seemed to want to say something. He put the whiskey to his lips, tipped his head back and swallowed.

Ambrose could see Tom wanted no part in this business. He was probably asking himself why he was involved in it all. There was Mr Danaher next door in his Aran jumper taking the clothes in and out from the line, his house impeccably clean. Why couldn't Tom have that sort of family, a big meal laid out for himself, his wife and children when they came down for a visit, scones and currant bread set on bone china?

Ambrose looked away and stared at his father. His father was impassive for the first time in years. He gazed at the wall, blinking occasionally. If he'd had his way, he'd have brought his hawthorn stick down on the table and ended this nonsense.

Nothing was the same. Ambrose noticed the room had been painted. Two onions had been skinned and set on the sill to absorb the odour of the paint, thirty years of grease vanquished with a bucket of water and a lick of paint. Ambrose shook his head. The carpet had also been replaced and the curtains washed. 'Oh, I see it all now, as if I didn't know what you were at all along,' Ambrose shouted, turning toward Tom and his mother. 'You're going to sell the place, that's it, isn't it?'

Tom took a step forward, his hands out as if he were going to lay them on Ambrose. 'Nothing has been decided . . . '

Ambrose raised his fist. 'She promised me this house,' he roared. 'After all I did for her . . . This is all I have. You won't do this to me!' Ambrose broke off and swallowed. His eyes gleamed. 'It's mine,' he whispered, his fists clenched. 'It's mine, make no mistake about it, Tom. She won't do this to me, after all I did. I swore I'd change and now you want to take this away from me, abandon me up in the mental home. Well, no way.' The whiskey bottle fell on its side, rolling back and forth and finally smashing on the floor. There was the sudden devastating silence of stifled tears and strained breath. Then Ambrose's father turned and blinked and said, 'I'm not going anywhere.'

Ambrose was shocked by his father's sudden words. His father turned his hard face on his thin neck and stared at the three of them. 'I'm not going anywhere,' he said again.

They were all flabbergasted for a moment, and then Tom put his hands deep into his pockets and looked at his mother.

'You're going to have to stay the night,' she whispered.

'I can't,' Tom answered.

'I'm here, Dad.' Ambrose put his hand on his father's shoulder.

Ambrose left the room without a word. He slept in his coat.

By the time Ambrose awoke the next morning, he had missed his medicine.

He felt terrible. The night had been humid. Rain had fallen in the early morning. He lay over the toilet bowl and tried to get sick. There was nothing in his stomach. He looked in the mirror for the first time in three days. On either side of his head, there were two patches of stubble where the electrodes had been placed. Ambrose touched the spots tentatively. This was where the electricity had entered his head. 'Christ,' he muttered. His looks were gone. Before, he'd always had a face that did not reconcile itself with the madness of his brain, an incongruity that could be masked. But now his face reflected the dismal state of his mind. He continued to wash but the soap kept slipping back into the cold water.

Ambrose dabbed himself dry. The left side of his face drooped slightly. He felt the numbness. The skin had an ashen look to it, devoid of blood, the flesh of the dead. There were sometimes complications with the shock treatment, nerve damage. Ambrose closed his eyes and sat down on the toilet for a moment, bringing his hands to his head. A strange melancholy filled him, and he shuddered, waiting with his trousers down around his ankles until the feeling left him.

What had they decided during the night? he wondered. Where would he go if they sold the house? His father's mild protest might have been forgotten. Who would listen to a sick man? After all these years, the sanctuary of home had become the only constant in his life. He'd given up on everything else, hiding in the house of his father, wasting his years in the company of his parents. He should have had the stability of a house for the rest of his life. He'd done it all for her, wrecked his life to give her money. At least his father had never asked him for anything, and here she was now, going to take it all away from him, to abandon her husband to a home and escape. Ambrose tensed in a spasm of anger and squirted piss against the bowl, like a creature instinctively protecting its territory.

There would be no escape for any of them. Ambrose pulled up his trousers. He went down and found his father back in the same old chair, although he could see that his shirt and trousers had been changed, and he'd been shaved, although he still had two scant tufts of hair on his cheekbones.

'Oh, you must be Ambrose,' a woman in a white nurse's uniform said, startled. She stood in the doorway before Ambrose.

Ambrose looked at her. 'Where's my mother?' he said.

'She's up at mass.' The nurse was a woman in her early thirties, heavy with a rounded face. Her hair was coiled up in a tight bun. A big nose detracted from her general attractiveness.

Ambrose bent down and looked at his father. 'Hello Dad.'

His father's blue eyes acknowledged him. Ambrose looked at the shiny head, seeing the contours of the skull, where the two plates of his father's skull had fused together. He was surprised that there were no visible marks on his father, no signs of physical injury. For a moment, Ambrose stared hard at him. His father looked away. Could his father have just gotten off his bicycle and just lain down in the ditch? He dismissed the notion before he'd conceived it, but his eyes still searched for some visible sign that his father had fallen down. 'When did he fall?' he heard himself asking.

'Two weeks ago. He's very weak.' The nurse came over beside Ambrose's father and touched his shoulder. 'He's on medication for heart trouble.'

Ambrose drew away to the table. The bottle of whiskey had been cleared away, although the carpet was still discoloured. 'My brother's gone then?' he asked.

'They left last night,' the nurse said.

Maybe he was overdressed in his officer's coat, but he felt a nakedness when he took it off after he'd worn it for extended periods. He was conscious of the weight he'd put on. The coat hid his corpulence, or so he thought anyway. He had developed a habit of keeping his coat on out in the lighthouse. It gave a look of activity, like he was a man on his way somewhere. People cut short their jabbering around him, acknowledging his urgency, or so he thought.

Ambrose felt dismayed still by the thin angular face of his father, the wrinkles gone because there was so little flesh on the body. He looked like an aged dummy that some ventriloquist had abandoned. He would never be the same again. In the three months' absence, his father had deteriorated in a way that should have taken years. He was closer to death than Ambrose could ever have imagined. If Ambrose stayed, it would be a stagnant waiting game, filled with life's most indecent moments, the sudden intimacy of a son cradling his father over a toilet bowl, taking a tissue to him without making eye contact, dressing him, taking the scarecrow arms and inserting them into cool, damp cotton shirts, fixing his tie, lacing his shoes.

'Would you like tea?' the nurse said, beaming a friendly smile.

'Yes, please,' Ambrose said.

'That fire never took.' She nodded at the wisps of smoke coming out of the grate.

'Leave it to me.' Ambrose smiled, but he felt ashamed of his own appearance. If he'd known there was someone downstairs, he'd have made a better showing of himself.

Ambrose watched her leave. She had thick legs, big calves inside the opaque of her stockings, like packed meat up at Munster Meats. An agricultural breed of woman, big boned and friendly, good for the easy kind of talk and intimacy that came with taking care of the sick. Her ruddy complexion had an apple's polish when she smiled back at him. Maybe she saw infirmity in him, a diviner drawn to the sick and lonely.

Ambrose looked away to the dead fire. His mother must have told her all about him, like she had told everybody else. She loved to flaunt her burdens, having the priest announce that this and that mass was for Ambrose who was up in Dublin at the hospital. Oh, yes, everybody knew of her sorrows.

Ambrose hunched over and rolled up a newspaper into tight balls and stacked them under the grate, packing some of the previous day's embers on top. Then he took a loose unfolded sheet and, holding it delicately between his fingertips, put it over the mouth of the fireplace. The paper wavered until a draught inhaled it gently against the mouth.

Ambrose kept his face at a safe distance. The paper browned in a scorch mark and then ignited into flames. Ambrose let go of the paper as it was sucked up the chimney.

The nurse came and stood at the door. 'Do you take sugar?'

'No.'

'The kettle's on,' she said.

'What's your name?' Ambrose asked, wiping his hands on his coat when the nurse came back in.

'Mary Conlin. Sorry, I didn't tell you. I forgot. Call me Mary.' She smiled, and her upper lip curled up to almost tip her big nose.

'And you can call me Ambrose.'

Mary moved her head in acknowledgment, almost embarrassment, and said, 'Oh, you got the fire going. Fires are very temperamental. You have to know what you're doing with them.'

'I suppose that's true. I wouldn't know. I'm not in the business of lighting other people's fires.' Ambrose made a pleasant face.

'Well I assure you I have had enough trouble with them in my time.' She showed pink gums when she smiled.

'That fire needs a good draught to get it started. There's no real secret to it,' Ambrose answered. He felt a sudden easiness in the ugliness of her smile. He had a love for this sort of half-beauty. Now that the fire talk had been exhausted, Ambrose nodded at his father and said, 'You know he was a great man in his time.' He sensed this lugubrious sentimentality was something that Mary Conlin longed for. She might even be the kind of catch Ambrose could get himself if he wanted and played his cards right, and now that he was considering settling down to a life of mediocrity, why not a good wife and some children? Why not, indeed?

'God love him,' Mary smiled, her thick fingers resting on the small ridge of her slightly protruding stomach. As she moved in the light, Ambrose could see through the semi-transparent white of her uniform, her bra and underwear strapped into place by inch-wide bands of elastic. He'd often wondered why white was the colour of medicine, the ominous prospect of blood on white.

The kettle whistle pierced the subdued morning air. 'I'll get the tea, then,' Mary said, leaving the room.

Ambrose's father tapped the arm of his chair. 'Go easy. That's my help there.'

Ambrose looked at him and smiled. It was the first real acknowledgment that his father could understand everything. Again, Ambrose had the strange feeling that his father had gotten off his bicycle and lain down in the ditch. It was an absurd notion, but he felt it all the same.

Mary Conlin came back moments later with slices of brown bread and tea on a tray and some porridge for Ambrose's father.

'That's great.' Ambrose rubbed his hands together. He took his cup of tea to his mouth and then cradled it in his lap.

Mary took a chair and sat before Ambrose's father, tucking a cloth in at his neck.

'My brother was saying that he couldn't be taken care of here. He looks all right to me,' Ambrose said. 'I mean there's not a scratch on him.'

Mary had set the small tray beside her on its thin metal legs. She was concentrating on Ambrose's father. There was a jar of honey beside the porridge. 'You'd like honey, Mr Feeney, wouldn't you?'

Ambrose's father nodded his head. Mary took a spoon, dipped it and then turned the spoon as the honey dripped into the porridge. The light caught the amber glob trickling off the spoon.

Ambrose persisted. 'Did my mother say anything about selling the house?' His voice had a faint tremor of excitement in it. He knew Mary detected it. She would not look at him directly, asking Ambrose's father questions, dabbing at the dribble of food at the edge of his lips. 'That's not too hot, is it, Mr Feeney?' She hunched forward, smiling.

'Did you hear she's thinking of selling the place?' Ambrose muttered again, squeezing his fingers around the striped blue mug that his father had always used to dip thick slices of toast.

'I really couldn't say,' Mary finally answered. She fed Ambrose's father without saying another word to Ambrose, concentrating on her duties.

Ambrose frowned. He shouldn't have started in about his mother. Things had been going fine. The last thing he wanted was to alienate Mary. Jesus, he couldn't take care of his father, that was for sure. If his people got a bad reputation, then it would be all off, and there'd be no chance of his father staying at home. Ambrose's mother would have her way. 'It looks like rain,' Ambrose said in a genial manner, rising. 'This tea is grand altogether. Do you scald the cup first?' A magpie hopped around the garden, then stopped and bobbed for worms.

'Scald the cup,' was all he got for an answer. Mary took the tray into the kitchen.

Ambrose's father looked at Ambrose with the soft blue eyes of old age. 'I'm going nowhere,' he said, putting out his

187

hand and taking Ambrose's hand. 'Don't do anything to that one, do you hear me?' his father whispered.

Ambrose went and stood in the kitchen in his long coat. He was still in his bare feet. 'Scalding the cup is the only way to make a good cup of tea,' he persisted.

'I have some work to get done,' Mary said, not turning around, fumbling with some pots. She had a small watch pinned to her uniform which she pretended to look at.

'I hope I didn't say anything . . . ' Ambrose stopped himself and went in to his father. He looked at him for a moment and felt there was something missing. He wrinkled his brow and looked again. 'Where are your medals?' Ambrose said to his father. His father didn't answer him. He had his head back, resting, his eyes closed.

Ambrose asked Mary the same question.

'What medals?' Mary answered, not turning to face Ambrose.

The medals he had on last night, and the scroll they had on the wall behind him.

'I don't know what you're talking about, Mr Feeney.'

'Ambrose, it's Ambrose, please.' Ambrose climbed the stairs. He stopped and caught his breath on the landing, standing under the bulb hanging from the ceiling with the shade that looked like one of his mother's hats. He went into the bathroom and stripped, filling the sink, and began to wash himself from head to toe.

Ambrose went into his room and waited for the bell for the next mass, knowing his mother would be home with a few ribs and potatoes for the dinner.

His mother came in with her hat and coat on, and Ambrose stood at the top of the stairs dressed in a clean new uniform, his face shaved and his body smelling of Old Spice.

Mary Conlin must have smelt the cologne because she looked up and saw him. Mary let Ambrose's mother into the hallway. 'How is he?' she whispered.

Ambrose came down the stairs. His mother looked up at him. 'I said a prayer that everything would work out.' She seemed short of breath, her small lips moving rapidly as she spoke. She handed over the bag of messages to Mary.

'I need to speak with you, Mam,' Ambrose said softly.

Mary Conlin looked at Ambrose's mother who moved her eyes about.

'Let's talk in here,' his mother answered.

The two of them sat in a damp room never heated, a small room of memorabilia, the sideboard filled with the black and white photographs of all the relatives. Ambrose could see that his mother had begun her business with the crayons on one of her own wedding photographs.

Ambrose went to the unused fireplace. It could easily have been evening the way the light filtered through the orange curtains. The road was silent outside. He tried to keep his composure, but couldn't stop the perspiration that plagued him. The shock treatment had done something to his internal thermostat.

Mary Conlin came in and set a saucer with hot milk and three tablets down beside Ambrose's mother. She raised her eyebrows, as if to say, 'Are you all right, Mrs Feeney?' Then she went out and shut the door softly.

'We could keep Mary on,' Ambrose began, 'and then we could stay here, all of us.'

Ambrose's mother said nothing, sitting resolutely stiff with the cup in her lap.

'I don't think I could go on without all of this, Mam,' Ambrose trembled. His Adam's apple bobbed in his throat. 'I swear I can change. All that business up in Dublin is over and through with.' Ambrose crossed his arms and then drew them apart. He spoke in a slow, deliberate manner, controlling the urge to plead. 'Finished, Mam. With Mary here in the mornings we can get on fine. You heard him say he was going nowhere himself, isn't that right, Mam?'

'It is, Ambrose.' His mother's false teeth seemed to hurt her and she dislodged them with a soft clicking sound over her mottled gums. 'Where will we get the money?' she whispered. 'It's very dear for a nurse.' She shifted forward and took the tablets from the saucer and put them into her mouth, skimmed away a thin skin on the milk, pinched it with her fingers and put in on the saucer and drank.

Ambrose watched her swallow, her eyes closed as she drank. He waited for her to put the glass back down on the saucer and stepping forward, tipped over and took the saucer from her lap, whispering, 'I have money, Mam. We'll use my money.'

His mother put a liver-spotted hand on Ambrose's arm and made the sign of the cross with her other hand, moving her thumb. 'Father, Son . . . Holy Ghost.' Ambrose whispered in unison.

'It has to be your decision,' she whispered, her wrinkled face pressed close to his. 'I want you to think of everything that you have said and called me all these years before you do anything. I'm too old for all of this.'

Ambrose began to weep. He knelt down and held his mother's hands. 'I want to do it for you,' he said, his head buried in her lap.

'I want you to do it for yourself, son,' she answered.

With this pact Ambrose gave his mother an installment of 40 pounds for four masses offered up at St Joseph's for the intentions of the family, and the private intention that Ambrose keep his hands off his mother and all concerned. Ambrose let it all pass unperturbed. It had come full circle. Why not a dose of religion again? He'd tried medicine.

As he held his mother's hand he looked up and whispered, 'Where are his medals?'

His mother answered, 'Safe. They're safe.'

'Safe, where?' Ambrose said.

Somewhere in the years between Ambrose's lunacy and his return home, man had landed on the moon. The distance between his enclosed world and the outside stretched, not continents, but planets. He was now Ambrose Feeney, Limerick man, Irish man, Earth man. Humanity's escape route had been plotted into the void of galaxies while Ambrose was still stuck in Limerick. The two world wars which had beset the early half of the twentieth century had been forgotten. Nuclear annihilation had been avoided. Ambrose had always harboured the feeling that annihilation was at hand. He'd considered the death of the Manchester United team an omen of the end. Everything had been grounded in his belief that the world would end in nuclear holocaust. Now the joke was on him, if it could be called a joke. Of all the children born in the year of his birth, Ambrose felt that none could have been more pathetic than himself. The supreme optimism of humanity had recovered and put history where it should be, in the past, and he had sat around with his smug doomsday satisfaction and waited for the world to end. Who could he blame?

Ambrose had been home a few months. The threat of war with England had dissipated. The North was in for a long-standing guerrilla campaign. Losses could be estimated. Troops were deployed and budgeted for. Anglo-Irish animosity could seethe in a controlled environment. This was the way the world was going to exist now, violence was an inherent part of humanity, curbed to smaller theatres, wars by proxy, Americans and Soviets fighting ideological battles, the Bay of Pigs, Vietnam, Jews and Egyptians and their Seven Day War, the occasional hunger striker up in H-Block. Violence manifest in wars of symbolism. Behind every war, negotiators worked in the United Nations and made secret deals and decided how much longer this and that struggle could be maintained.

Ambrose was lying in bed in his suit and tie, dodging the world, waiting in the sanctuary of dark. He had resumed the quiet mania of his former years, a prisoner inside himself, sleeping as much as possible to make life pass, preserving as much detachment as he could during his waking encounters with the world.

Next door to Ambrose, his mother slept. His father was still downstairs in the front room, and Mary Conlin, whom he thought might have married him, slept upstairs in the room next to his mother. She had three locks on her door which set the tone for her relationship with Ambrose after he'd made suggestions about a film he thought she might like to see. An overture of chocolates and flowers had also been rejected by this 'boiled-ham-faced fucker', as Ambrose called her. They were not on speaking terms other than, 'Will you have tea?' and he'd respond, 'I will. Thank you very much.' There were still boxes of chocolates with ribbons downstairs which he had bought for Mary Conlin. His mother would rifle through them some nights when she was in need of a few sweets.

The clock rang and Ambrose got up and sat at the edge of the bed. The city outside had settled down hours before. The ship out on the estuary was moving through the darkness, passing silent houses. People stayed up all night, in other cities, roaming warm streets in loose clothing, but Limerick curled into itself when darkness descended. Even a fire in the grate could not give reprieve from the cold.

This coldness added to the general malignancy. If it had been colder, an Arctic winter with snow, then something would have been done. People would have built proper houses and dressed warmly. But in Limerick the coldness only nagged. It was treated with irksome familiarity, the troublesome child, people standing around and complaining about it in doorways. 'Oh, the weather,' the women would say under their breaths as the sky moved overhead, how a shower soaked the clothes on the line, how the holiday was wrecked. The city was full of men hunched on bicycles, wavering as they pedalled into rain and wind, men who walked around with damp clothes on their backs that smelt of rain and sweat. There was no sense of conquering, only living with what the weather brought. Half-measures sufficed, an old coat or heavy jumper, a hot-water bottle for the feet, a cup of tea before bedtime. Once you were born into this way of thinking, this mystifying benign way, on the verge of re-cognition, with a mulling disposition, but in the realm of indecision, there was no hope for you. Ambrose knew this only too well. Mediocrity loves misery. Ambrose wiggled his toes and looked for his shoes which he found. He went downstairs and put on the kettle so he could waste time and warm his body. He walked into the sitting room. Mary Conlin had set the table for breakfast, the cups turned over on the saucers. She had everything planned as though if something happened to her, if she died during the night, at least breakfast wouldn't be disturbed.

Ambrose went out of the sitting room and took the kettle off the boil before it whistled, not wanting to wake anybody, and made a pot of tea. He waited silently. He walked down the narrow passage to the back door, opened it and checked the weather. A cloudy sky drifted overhead, the moon appearing and disappearing. His bicycle slept in the shed. He took it out, wheeled it into the kitchen and pumped up the tyres for want of something to do.

When Ambrose turned to get the tea off the cooker, his father was standing there before him in his pajamas. He looked at Ambrose with longing, as though remembering the old days when he could take his own bicycle out into the night and lose himself in hard exercise.

'I'll bring you in tea if you want,' Ambrose said. He put the pump down beside the bicycle.

'Do you have a puncture?' his father asked.

'I'm just keeping air in them,' Ambrose answered.

'You're making tea?'

'I am. You'll have a cup?'

'I will,' his father said.

'I'll bring it in to you, if you want?' Ambrose straightened himself, the pump still in his left hand.

'I don't want to lie in that bed anymore,' his father said obstinately. His voice had a weak shakiness to it. He sat down at the table and cradled his arms.

'I'll bring the heater in if you're staying put.'

'Leave it,' Ambrose's father said. He breathed hard, his thin head moving slowly in the greyish light.

Ambrose looked at the floor. He saw his father's feet were bare. He went out of the room and came back with a pair of slippers and knelt down before his father. His father moved his feet, giving them up like a horse getting shod. Ambrose took each foot by the ankle and slowly set it into the slipper. When Ambrose stood up, he felt a rush of blood to his head. He had to lean against the warm metal of the cooker to regain his balance.

His father's eyes shifted in his head, but he said nothing as Ambrose recovered himself. 'We'll have tea, then,' Ambrose whispered.

A street lamp outside and the moon gave off the only luminescence to the kitchen. Ambrose, as his father had always done, liked to sit in semi-darkness, a nocturnal serenity where everything he did was a mere ghost of movement, the braille intimacy of knowing one room, hands moving with the foreknowledge of everything. Ambrose had always been conscious of his father's ability to stay motionless for hours. Nothing was wasted. Ambrose had been conscious of that much all through his life. His father's economy wasn't frugality in the sense of meanness. There were just things that were not needed. If you sat in the darkness long enough, your eyes adjusted.

His father, when he'd been in good health, used to sit silently, drinking black tea, his fingers scanning the table for crumbs which he brought to his mouth. He wouldn't cut more bread until the table had been licked clean. When Ambrose was younger, he had asked his father why he sat in the darkness. His father had told him of how during the war people had become used to the blackouts and not long before that, there had been no electric light. His father said that he'd always found it blinding anyway. Ambrose had followed his father's habit and discovered a secret part of life that could only be lived in darkness, the soothing dimension of shadow forms moving before his eyes. Now this enigmatic starkness had entered his father's head in the form of senility, the forgetfulness of things around him, names, people, objects and places. And the hardening of the arteries had begun inside him too, the slow process toward the inanimate, a consenting to the nothingness there in the kitchen which had sustained him for so many years. Ambrose looked at his father's thin body hunched forward against the table. He wanted to say something, to try and open up some form of communication with him, especially on these lonesome nights since he'd returned from the institution. He almost touched his father but didn't. His father preserved his habitual blankness, not allowing words to penetrate. To simply exist was enough for his father. He seemed to have discovered Cartesian philosophy all by himself, 'I think, therefore, I am.'

Ambrose poured the tea into the two cups, took a bottle of milk out of a can of cold rainwater and added a sup of milk to his tea for colour's sake. His father's hand hovered over his cup, as though he was afraid Ambrose was going to pour milk into his tea which Ambrose never had done in all his life, and yet his father had this animal mistrust. Ambrose watched his father and put the milk back into the can, and his father removed his hand, damp from the steam, and wiped it on his pajamas.

They drank in silence, both staring at the bicycle which stood in the middle of the kitchen, a third presence.

Ambrose looked at his watch, straining in the light coming into the kitchen.

197

His father unhooked his finger from the ear of his cup. 'You'll be going then?'

Ambrose looked at his father. 'The tide should be up soon.'

His father hesitated and then went back to his tea, brought it to his lips, but then set it down without drinking it. He touched Ambrose on the arm. Ambrose felt the slight throb of pressure, his father's body trembling. 'It's a terrible thing,' his father whispered. His head moved in the greyness, inching closer than it had ever come to Ambrose in all his years.

Ambrose stiffened and put his cup down. He let his father's weight rest on his arm. 'What?' he said softly.

'Some things that I've seen . . . they had to be done . . . had to be done . . . but terrible all the same.' His father closed his eyes, his head nodding to himself. His breath had an acrid smell from the black tea and the sickness. He turned away, letting go of Ambrose's arm.

'I saw a vet do something horrible to an animal once . . . ' His father kept his head down, the dismal silence shared between them.

Ambrose stiffened at the unimaginable, at what his father could have been talking about, a man who had sat into the night sharpening his knives.

His father breathed in a trembling way. He seemed as though he was about to get up, but didn't. The thread of some thought unwound in his head and he whispered, 'Terrible things I've seen . . . '

Ambrose closed his eyes, the dark confessional intimacy of thoughts spun through a loom of whispered ellipses. His father had arrived at that point where the provisional darkness of his room had now become like the horrible confinement of a grave, each waking moment, each pose like trying a still death repose.

His father opened up his hands and then laced them together again around his tepid tea. He drank slowly, wiping his sleeve across his lips after every mouthful. He touched Ambrose's hand again, the need to feel human flesh.

Ambrose didn't dare speak. His father was talking of more than animals. What terrible things could happen to a man who had eaten his own slaughter all his life. Ambrose had seen this bleak fatalism before, the unconscious atheism, but back then his father could take out his knives and whittle away the silver filings until the blade gleamed, and his arm hung, fagged with effort. The stasis of these small rooms dogged his father in his dying days. Work which had provided a living had provided a refuge from life. The hours spent in gathering animals together, getting up at the crack of dawn all those years, attending to animal needs which were less demanding than human needs, but non-negotiable. The animals were there, with that farm-animal consciousness, coming around a man, butting him, snorting, demanding things from him. The silent compact of slaughter had been set down from the moment a farmer pulled a bonamh from a sow or a calf from a cow in a cold shed.

The toilet flushed upstairs. Ambrose's father hesitated. 'That farm should have been mine.' His head bobbed in the darkness. The disinherited feeling of all those years out on the road, killing another's animals, had ended in this house. He had been conceived in a bed, in a room, in a house, on a farm, his father's house on his father's farm. That he could under-stand. But now he was dying in a bed, in a house, on a street, in a city and he felt the vacancy of owning nothing – no animals, no farm, no land. The house would be sold after his death, there was no succession, only abandonment. His children had already left Limerick and were off in different cities, in different countries. Some of them would not even be able to come home for his death.

A loose rain rapped against the window. It broke the mood. The moonlight was gone. Ambrose got up and turned on the light in the hall. 'I'm cold,' his father whispered.

His father laboured to get up, shifting about in his slippers. The hard plastic soles scraped across the concrete floor. 'I want you to do something for me,' his father whispered, pointing at Ambrose.

Ambrose tilted forward, straining to listen. Ambrose could hear movement on the landing upstairs and put a finger to his lips.

'Is that you, Ambrose?' Ambrose's mother croaked. 'Are you off then?'

'I'm off,' Ambrose whispered and then turned off the light in the hall. He and his father went into the front room where his father slept and Ambrose shut the door. The room held a pocket of damp heat. A small bed of slack glowed in the fireplace. Everything was cramped, the bed taking up so much of the small room, the family photographs huddled onto a sideboard along with his father's medicine bottles, ointments, a cup of water, a thermometer, a small statue of St Joseph, rosary beads and a worn bible.

'I want to be buried with my medals,' his father said.

His father remained standing near the fire, although he retracted his hands and just stood motionless, like one of his animals abandoned in the darkness, waiting patiently for something to happen.

Ambrose had the premonition that his father had lain down

out there on the road when he was up in the institution, that he'd set himself down in a ditch in a moment of supreme animalism. How does a man who ended other lives end his own?

'You'll have your medals,' Ambrose said with decided firmness.

His father turned and looked at Ambrose with his drawn face, his eyes cavernous, lost in the dimness of the room. Ambrose could not see them, but felt them on him. 'Terrible things were done for this country. Terrible things had to be done.'

His father's lips moved mutely, the first acknowledgment of something passing silently in the darkness. He had done something during the war. Ambrose had listened to his father at night with the radio on, tuned into the conflict over the North since he'd come home. His father had always been for a united Ireland. To be buried in his medals was all he could hope for. At the end of his life, it wasn't that he feared damnation, as much as his suffering meant nothing, the insinuating feeling that it had all been in vain. His terrible memories would stay only with him. He could say nothing about it at the end of his life.

'All the real battles were fought by you and men like you,' Ambrose said. 'It was all part of the same war.' He touched his father gently.

Ambrose's father slumped down on the bed. He didn't look up. 'Part of the same war.' His father seemed to try to bring this image into his head, to align it with what he had done. Once he had that, this seam between himself and the greater violence, he could see its progression. The hardest thing in the world is for a man to be left with irrational action.

If meaning can be put on the worst atrocities, then there can be crusades, grand inquisitions, genocide and atomic bombs and men who go to the grave with no fear of damnation. 'Part of the same thing,' Ambrose's father muttered to himself as Ambrose knelt before him, taking each ankle and removing the slippers. On one phrase the meaning of life could stand, it was different for each man, but it always began with a simple sentence, a sentence like, 'In the beginning . . .' which implies an end. In this all actions were endowed with meaning, there was not a moment of excess in life, the supreme economy of living had a honed realism befitting creation by a god.

Ambrose wheeled his bicycle into the hall. A thin bar of light streamed from under his father's door, washing over his feet. Ambrose stood outside. He didn't know if he should go in again. Instead, he got a chair from beside the statue of St Philomena, and stood up on it, feeding four ten pences into the box so there would be electricity for the morning's breakfast. Then he opened the front door and left.

The night frost had settled on the grass and the tops of the walls. Ambrose pulled his collar tight to his neck. His father was at the window. Ambrose wheeled the bicycle through the garden with its barren bushes waiting to bear another season's adoration of flowers. As he closed the garden gate, Ambrose looked up and could see his father still moving behind the curtain.

Ambrose did not get on the bicycle. He put his hand on the seat and steered the bicycle up the road, breathing hard as he went. Then he stopped at the top of the road, set the bicycle against a wall and cried out loud.

In the city his bicycle moved silently through the dimly lit street. He was still pushing it, the front wheel weaving a little, as though looking at things with Ambrose. Ambrose knew you were in a bad way when you anthropomorphized a bicycle, when you were afraid to jump up on the seat. He went on, himself and his bicycle. He passed the crumbling Limerick siege walls always smelling of organic dampness. The city had been a series of walls within walls through the years, grim fortresses for hidden people.

His head was bad, maybe even worse than it had been in years. He'd abandoned the tablets he'd been prescribed, fearing that maybe his illness was sustained by them, being dependent on something always. He wished he had the tablets now. He had to calm himself down.

The road gleamed as he passed under a patch of bad frost in a narrow lane. He was almost plodding to make sure that his legs didn't slide from under him. The sky hung with a heavy misty rain, dampening Ambrose's face and hands as he moved. He found it hard to manoeuvre the bicycle. His hand kept shaking with the cold and the memory of his father back in the bedroom. At the top of the street, a dog came out and sniffed Ambrose's leg, nosed the bicycle and then moved off down the road.

Ambrose was already late for the shipping vessels. They would have docked and the captains would be waiting for him, but he couldn't bring himself to get up on his bicycle and get down there quickly. He stopped and set the bicycle up against a wall and left it there, walking away from it without looking back. He'd get it later. He needed solitude just now.

He went on down by St John's church, past the small houses, his body hemmed in by narrow meandering lanes, houses built into the walls on some streets, a concrete atavism going back to the cavemen. The concrete facades had small slit windows barely letting in light. For years he had walked among these lanes, seeing faces of old men and women sitting in the hall or at the edge of a door, put out to get a bit of air, dressed warmly in black to absorb what little heat trickled down from the sun. In the day, people moved them inside like phantoms, the small windows draped with a thin white curtain or adorned with bowls of plastic fruit or a little statue. Ambrose had read somewhere that there had once been a window tax imposed on the size and number of windows in a house, and so here it was now, a siege consciousness, a people moving like moles in the darkness of their own homes, not remembering that it was military oppression that had dictated the geometry of their houses, military oppression that made them creep around in the step-down crypts of cold rooms, living in the facade of the walls that imprisoned them.

It was all prison as far as Ambrose was concerned, the morose feeling that lends itself to despair, feelings lying below consciousness that only the lucidity of darkness can penetrate for a moment, an architecture built out of people's fears. Into lanes of darkness Limerick had crept, from green fields to brick, bringing its slaughter into its domain, into small houses where you bent your head going in through the doorway. Disaffection had become so daunting at some point, so omnivorous that to stave it off, one thought in terms of only the present, what will I eat, what can I eat, where will I buy it, when will I buy it, how will I cook it, what will I drink with it . . . And this one trick was applied to each meal, three times a day, the religiosity of three, of ritual, elemental concerns bringing out the most contrived but immanently safe plans, the illusion of movement preserved in stasis, the bad weather thrown in for good measure, the element of chance, caught in a shower, stranded in a door front with bags full of the next meal to be consumed, only two hours away and the time pressing on.

Ambrose could see that too many memories were invoked in stone which possesses nothing really. It was man who, in reworking the old masonry through the centuries, created a labour of baroque despair, indecipherable histories which meant nothing, jumbled into half-stories of what the people had been once.

Ambrose heard the throaty coo of pigeons tucked into holes in the walls where the stones had become dislodged. Bits of corrugated roof hung over other parts of the walls as he went along, old cars set up on blocks, reeking of congealed oil, horses in another yard facing a wall, tethered to steel rings, the rich odour of damp horse hair and clumps of manure palpable.

Ambrose pushed on, wanting to reach the wide-open square by the church. He tried to move faster, but his feet would not respond. He moved along, panting, his shoes echoing in the dirty lane, the slur of the night's rain in the sloping drains. Shadows lay on shadows, patches of ice gleaming on the road where rays of moonlight shone through breaches in the wall from some battle or struggle through the years. He stopped at a house that had been half-burnt a few years ago, the vacant stillness, reminiscent of life, the bleached floral wallpaper still visible on some of the walls, the fireplace filled with bricks, a chair set on its side, stairs rising up into night, to where a second storey had once been. Ambrose looked at the stairs leading nowhere. How many things had been created when the end was long gone, archeologists unearthing the remains of roads to extinct cities?

Ambrose looked at the pitch sky, a victim of this city of sieges too, sharing a need for confinement and walls, confining himself to the mental institution which was after all a more attenuated imprisonment than anything before him, having to seek prison out, an artificial hibernation of enclosure, to mimic what his people had been forced to live within for generations. Was there ever a generation that had the burden of trying to imprison itself like he was forced into now? Ambrose finally came out into the open square, the cold full moon casting his shadow to twice his length as he walked on.

By the edge of the Shannon, Ambrose passed St John's castle with its walls dipping into water. The first settlers had arrived by water on the Shannon banks. Ambrose went on up by the docks, past the prostitutes standing up against the walls, creatures with long legs exaggerated by stiletto heels and fish-net stockings. Ambrose usually had his bicycle and glided past them, but now on foot, they came out from the shadows, approaching him, saw the uniform and recoiled back under stone.

In the murkiness of night, ships bobbed on the water's edge, the moon anchored in darkness, the sky another ocean. Ambrose buried his hands in his pockets, pushing on. In this refracted light, eyes glimmered, jewelry glittered, the reel of sexual tension had been cast into the blackness, a fly spinning, descending into deep water. Ambrose heard a car putter on the cobblestones, saw the red tail-lights seething with lust. A door opened ahead of him, the stark aquatic light of a fish tank. Ambrose could sense the primordial instinct to reproduce, the appeal of those long legs of the prostitute as she leaned into a window, the shapely flagella of swimming cells thrashing through the viscosity of ocean floors. No wonder men were reduced to whistling, primitive recognition, a distant mating call. He felt the throb in his own groin. Prostitutes and their customers were drawn to water, the spawn of desire propagating itself amidst the aroma of grizzled pubic hair like seaweed, the slime of lubrication, semen tasting of salt, the tight little universes of DNA knotted in discarded condoms in the early dawn.

Ambrose had come somehow in his life to stand at the edge of this dock where everything either came or left the city. Ambrose moved quietly, conscious of his own virginity for the first time, of having produced nothing. He resisted the impulse to stop and disappear into the wall, to lose the ludicrous stigma. All he could think of was his mother's statue of the Virgin Mary. A chill went through him. He had unwittingly put himself into that realm of martyrdom for his mother at the beginning of his life, and had entered into celibacy after the institution. He had lived amid purveyors of pornography these past years, working alongside the customs officers, watching them seeking it out on ships, removing magazines in bags, taking them to the bins out the back of the customs house and burning them. And before that he had sat among the rocks on the edge of the sea before they came and took him to the institution. He had lingered too long at the source of life and death, too long an interloper on the banks of a stinking river in his home town.

A gigantic Polish Coal Ship loomed alongside him, an ominous buttress of grey metal, sailors speaking in their foreign way. He understood none of it. He turned around and faced the long corridor of darkness and prostitutes, the isolated cars dimming their lights, purring beside the walls, the irredeemable abjectness of a sex-driven race. His head was bad, but he began walking into the irresistible darkness with his hands to his temples with the imperturbable certainty that he must abandon all things around him. What had been an answer for others had always been a question for him. He had lived too long among men and their histories. He was going inland, back into the heart of a city, into an institution, into a room without windows, without sun or moon, and he would begin again in his own way, delivered from temptation.

ONE OF THE MANY POST-MODERN UNCORRECTED BEGINNINGS FROM THE COLLECTED ABORTED FIRST BEGINNINGS OF AMBROSE'S FIRST GREAT UNFINISHED NOVEL:

The Burden of Influence

If Ambrose Feeney were to tell it straight now, he'd have to begin not at the beginning, but with a cup of tea and a bun. Ambrose could begin nothing without taking care of bodily functions first, a nice cup of tea and a bun.

Would he begin this story in the present or the past, in the cafeteria or with a childhood memory? He looked around the cafeteria and frowned. It had no real significance to his story. There was nothing to say about the cafeteria. Nothing mattered in the present. These things had not made him a lunatic.

Where to Begin?

With a disclaimer first and foremost.

This is written by a certifiably Committed Man.

The names and places have not been changed, because
nobody was innocent.

The records would show he never did anything of his own
volition. Even this text was mandated by the hospital, part of
therapy.

Maybe he should get a solicitor first. It would be good to
have the law involved. This sort of story was bound to create
a legal controversy among the relatives, maybe even death
threats. There were a couple of wasters who would be
watching him closely. The possibility thrilled him. A close
reading is all that a writer can beg for, to be taken seriously.
And here, with suit and counter suit, the text would be
imparted with all its attenuating meanings, a true literary
analysis, a text that spawns other texts. Ambrose was not so
megalomaniacal that he had to author everything. To be part
of the phenomenon, that was enough, with all things leading
back to his work.

At this stage, with nothing down on paper, Ambrose's
anxieties lay in volume, not content. He'd take care of
legalities when they arose, and with his presumed insanity he
was well couched from any serious consequences.

Foreword
This text is written by a certifiably Committed Man.

He liked the double-entendre of Committed. At least he was
above animal logic. Animals had happiness, hatred, sorrow,
but not irony.

An old cleaning woman in a navy blue pinafore pushed a

trembling trolley around the room, destroying his concentration. 'Fuckin bitch,' Ambrose growled. He set his eyes on her as she collected dirty cups and saucers, the shift of her fat bottom manoeuvring around the place. 'How are you this morning, pet? Can I get you a sup of tea, love?' She went on with condescending politeness among the mad women.

Ambrose looked at the group of women, unwashed, the smell of sleep under a layer of powder, suffering under the double affliction of depression and the change of life. Ambrose called them collectively, 'The Hormone Express'. He thanked God he was a man, that his penis was there in his trousers ready for personal inspection with his own eyes. The God-forsaken trepidation of those ol' ones having to exist with things going on unseen inside their bodies. Everything had to be felt with probing fingers, slight swelling of this or that. Ambrose turned away. The staleness of menopause, the palpable stench of mental illness added to his own heightened fear of decay. Women were menacing beasts. He left it at that. He took a deep ponderous breath, the kind men took before saying big things, or lies.

To Begin
I am a sick man . . . I am an angry man. I am an unattractive man.

Ambrose had originally planned to take a plastic biro in hand, one where he could see the ink running dry, to give urgency, or, more exactly, what he called, 'a laconic lucidity' to every word. A vein of veritable ink.

Ambrose was impressed with the staccato effect of his introduction, a clinical impunity, what will be said has its doubling effect, the confessional resonance of the 'I' juxtaposed with the word 'man' at the end of every sentence. Into this margin life comes to have meaning, between the personal and the social. And after all, that was the essence of his struggle.

'Holy mother of Jesus!' Ambrose was destroyed. He had actually duplicated the beginning of *Notes From Underground*. 'I am a sick man . . . I am an angry man. I am an unattractive man.' And he hadn't the nerve to argue probability. He checked other translations, but they were all firm in their opening lines. 'I am a sick man . . . I am an angry man. I am an unattractive man.' Ambrose cried to himself and paced out in the garden for days. It was not plagiarism, it was probability. A thesis on probability added to his own harrowing tale would have been too much for Ambrose. Maths was not his strong point. He'd have to modify the opening on any account.

To Begin Again
I am a sick Limerick man . . . I am an angry Limerick man. I am an unattractive Limerick man.

He was making progress with maximum effort but with little effect, the kind of inverse relationship that he had dreaded from the start. Place had to be set in time. It was part of the equation of plot, of life?

I am sick Limerick man . . . I am angry Limerick man. I am unattractive Limerick man, living in the aftermath of World War Two.

*

214

He put the pen down and rubbed his hands together. It was an arseways approach to getting anything done, a symptom of schizophrenia. He was feeling the parts of himself cleaving. The entire thing was beyond him. As the saying goes, 'He's not half the man his father is', well, you'd have to keep that division going for a while before you'd arrive at Ambrose. He saw the traits of his father in himself, but they now were so convoluted that none of it worked for him.

Forget the *Notes From Underground* beginning. Start over. His story wasn't set in Russia. His characters had simple names: Frank, Tom, Pat, Jim. Identifiable characters, their limits of moral insight were preordained by the places you would find one of these names, in pubs or in cold brick houses. Some had been pushed too far by Mr Joyce and Mr Beckett and all that stuff, but at least it went mostly unread by the common eejit. It left Ambrose in an impossible situation all the same. If he confronted any sort of problem in his fictive life, he'd be obliged to come up with queer sorts of drunkards, philosophical brutes in shoes without laces who argued the existence of good and evil.

Jasus, he wasn't even a drinker himself. He looked at the beginning again. God it was great stuff. Maybe his story was all alienation after all. If the unlaced shoe fits, wear it. Ambrose was in desperation with the names. He felt Russian literature's lucidity and skewed vision came from the more foreign sound of names like Tredyakovsky or Perevosh-chikov. Pronunciation stumbled into the sublime, creating the potential for alienation. Form and content merged exactly, the brain must send the message to the tongue and it must form the sounds of such long names, and into that sphere, those seconds of pronunciation, the subconscious can articulate more subtle or brooding people and literature. (Now if Ambrose would have known Russian, here would have been the place to prove his case.)

Now for an Irishman to get this ponderous expression, this philosophical tenor to his ways, there was only one thing for it: drink! For the seasoned drinker, the pint and a shot, the long and the short . . . brought out a sneering resolve in the men. They spoke or stumbled over words, and their bodies moved equally slowly in ponderous gestures, the head tipped back with the stout running into the funnel of the throat and then the lurch forward, the eyes, small watery slits opening, and a thought set in motion from the recesses of the head and sent flying downward to the mouth for expression.

Come to think of it now, the Russians had their vodka. Ambrose wondered if they practised 'rounds', as they called it in his place, whereby a man buys a drink for everyone in a group and all concerned keep drinking until everyone has bought everyone else a round. From Ambrose's vantage, a lifetime member of the pioneer association, he had formed the opinion that this practice allowed the most extreme element in any gathering the upper hand. The best and worst drinkers were wedded together, and in the end the country's future was decided upon by this extreme drinking element.

Still Ambrose wondered if the Russians found their own writers so despairing.

He was straying from his story. What he needed was a truly long Irish name for his main character, something longer than Murphy or Malone. To find new names, long Irish names, would be fair going, a sore hand from paging the telephone directory.

Ambrose had always had that kind of a way, even as a

child, dismantling everything to see how it worked: bicycles, train sets, the radio. It wasn't good enough that a clock told the time. He had to pry it open, letting his fingers go at the cogs. And with magic or card tricks, he went mad with anxiety, harassing magicians for the secret, for the subterfuge, fixated on the parts rather than the whole.

It was chronic unbelief, but at the time his parents called it fiddling.

Ambrose was a Fiddler.

Ambrose called himself a Deconstructionist in his most cynical moments, but a plain ballocks most of the time.

Ambrose Takes Time Off
to drink the cup of tea and eat a bun.

The cafeteria waited patiently for description. He came to it begrudgingly. He'd said all he wanted to say about it, but here he was now.

The cafeteria, a glass gazebo, extended to the edge of a green lawn, a hothouse edifice with potted plants hanging from a glass ceiling, nested in by small finches. It gave the illusion of nature but was pumped with the comfort of domestic gas heat. Tubes of stark fluorescence diffused an aura of enhanced light so that every time Ambrose entered the room he was blinded.

Ambrose called it 'an indoor Xanadu' in front of the relatives who came to see him on occasion. Everything was set out judiciously. The space between the tables was measured to let people talk in privacy, but not in isolation. Sound fell as muffled whispers. It could be tuned in or tuned out. It had a practical abstraction. And there was music drifting into the recesses of the gazebo that could never actually be heard.

Ambrose loved the aesthetics of that non-music, it compounded the anxiety of that pat feeling that so many lunatics complain of: hearing things in their heads. Still Ambrose spent hours in exercises where he tried to decipher intent from form, and if only he could have heard things in his head, it would have saved him from having to bore himself with his own questions.

The long and short of the gazebo was that on sunny days it roasted his arse, and for the rest of the time he was annoyed by the rain on the glass, harassed by a static that would drive the sane demented.

Sometimes Ambrose fed a finch a few crumbs of his bun, rounding out the symbiosis of the design. The architect would have been proud of him, man in harmony with the birds, fulfilling this conceptual Eden. The small finch had a nest in one of the light trays.

The women were at it again, chattering. Thank God they stayed in their half of the room, acknowledging the unspoken apartheid. Sex and madness, as bad as drinking and driving. Ambrose felt the description mount, useless to his story. He might as well go on, for the edification of God knows who. The gazebo was for visitors, for the women's families, the severe husbands smoking in the corridors, the daughters bringing balls of wool for the knitting, pictures of the grandchildren, neighbours' apple tarts, always a brimming optimism.

'She looks great, doesn't she?'

'Did they cut your hair? It looks lovely.'

'Let me tell you anyway who's going off to England, as if

we don't know what for . . . '

Ambrose sat in his chair looking over at the earnest face of a girl in her twenties holding her mother's hand, rubbing it gently. She was crying softly. The grandmother sat like an old crow in black, probably deaf, saying nothing.

'You'll be home for the christening . . . for Christmas . . . for your birthday . . . for Kitty's communion . . . ' Ad infinitum.

Ambrose had his hands to his face. 'Would you like more tea, Ambrose?' a small bandy-legged orderly asked. He was almost dwarfish. 'You're grand, there?'

Ambrose pointed to the rattling trolley, grimacing. The state was paying for his peace.

'Go easy, Bridie. Ambrose has a headache,' Frankie winked. 'Did you take your tablets, Ambrose?'

'No.'

'You'd like another cup then, Ambrose, to wash them down?'

'I would,' said Ambrose. 'And a cream bun, Frankie.' Ambrose watched Frankie go over to Bridie. She was fuming. They had been married for donkey's years and lived on the grounds of the hospital in what used to be the gatekeeper's lodge.

The hospital was almost like a luxury hotel, except for a faint smell of antiseptic. And there was no overt exchange of money. The tea was apparently free, and the buns, a confectioner's charity. But Ambrose knew that everything was totted up on a bill which was sent to the Voluntary Health. He knew the buns were costing a bomb, right enough. He thought to himself that the presiding governors of the ward must have felt that money was at the root of all mental illness.

As benevolent quasi-social Marxism ruled, a few quid on a policy and all was taken into account. Mental treatment shouldn't look like it was being administered at a charge in the hospital. It was one of those inalienable rights. Whatever the case, Ambrose thought the socialized buns were worth the price.

Ambrose gave up on anything productive now. His head was bad, messing with long Irish names to get that Russian aura.

Sean Malone eyed Ambrose. He sat down at the table with a nod and pointed to the orderly, 'Same again,' American-cowboy-style, and then burst out laughing.

Ambrose took the intrusion in his stride, with his head tilted to the side and his tongue working away on the cream filling. 'So it's the big day, then?'

'It is indeed, Ambrose,' Sean said, drumming his fingers on the table. Sean Malone was dressed in tan trousers and a navy blue jumper with a Trinity College crest. His family had sent in the clothes, pressed and starched.

'You could cut butter with that crease,' Ambrose said for the sake of talk.

'Oh right, that's a good one, Ambrose. The wife is particular to a fault.'

Sean was on the verge of baldness. He had two wings of grey wispy hair matted and damp against his skull. His forehead was his most prominent feature, an expanse of furrowed anxiety that rippled up to the crown of his head. He looked helpless enough, a tall man. The gangliness of his sporting days had fallen to the corruption of age.

'The big day. Please God, the weather should hold for you,' Ambrose looked up through the gazebo.

'I told them I wouldn't leave on a rainy day. Too depressing, driving home with the windows damp and all that sort of thing.'

'The weather should hold all right for you,' Ambrose smiled.

'You'll be starting back at the school soon, I suppose?'

Sean licked his dry lips. The shock treatment seemed to have taken the moistness out of his spit, as though he had a mouthful of cotton wool. 'I don't know yet. I'll have to have a go at the garden first when I get back. It's time the soil was turned for the planting.'

Ambrose swallowed. 'You know best, Sean. There's no need to rush into anything at all. The world has got on fine without us.'

'I've been thinking about ending it all back at the house. I wouldn't do it here, of course,' Sean whispered.

Ambrose shook his head. 'Come on, Sean. We had some good times. You have a lovely wife, and didn't you say your daughter was getting married soon?'

'Jesus, obligations, obligations. And the bridegroom's father, yours truly, pays for all that. And I'm stuck with four girls, mind you.' Then Sean shrugged his shoulders. 'Well anyway, Ambrose, you'd better look me up when you decide to give up the game.' Sean forced his lips into a smile.

Sean had been the first professed atheist that Ambrose had come across after his arrival, and, to say the least, Ambrose had been disappointed with the ordinariness of what had been billed an 'Anti-Christ.'

Ambrose and Sean shared a room. The entrance committee paired patients according to the severity of their illness, their religious affiliation, and their level of personal hygiene. When

221

asked what he thought about religion on the entrance questionnaire, Ambrose had answered that he 'didn't give a flying fuck about religion'. He envisioned God, if he was forced to do so, as 'a monkey with a mallet up its arse'. That seemed to constitute atheism. Sometimes Ambrose would look at Sean sleeping and say to himself, 'So this is how bad they think I am.'

Sean had that agitated look about him, the dull pastiness of his face, the blanched lips on the verge of saying something. He was shivering. The after-effects of the shock treatment still lingered with all of them. The staff had made him bathe to get rid of the smell of the ammonia of sickness from the incontinence. Odour was a form of mental illness. His daughters were coming to take him home later in the morning.

'You have cream on your nose,' Sean said, his face furrowed. His skin was red from the cold water.

Ambrose let his tongue probe his nose.

Sean reeked of cheap aftershave.

'How's she this morning?' Sean looked up to the tray where the finch had her eggs.

'She's grand. Ate a few crumbs,' Ambrose answered. 'She's getting fat.'

'I'd love to stay on . . . I mean, to see the eggs hatch . . . ' Sean pinched the bridge of his nose. 'I'm not well,' he whispered, leaning toward Ambrose. 'I don't want to go back out there. But . . . '

'What?' Ambrose whispered.

'The benefits are running out. I don't want her to have to sell the house for my sake.'

Ambrose looked mechanically to the outside. There was a

fine par three golf course that ran down to the back garden walls laced with coils of barbed wire and cemented with fins of glass. The staff insisted at orientation that the wire and glass were to keep people from the outside from coming in to play a few holes. A group of patients was setting up to tee off. Ambrose was amazed that patients were allowed to have clubs, as if their mental illness was not something so vicious that they would turn around and start smashing someone's head open. He was ashamed of himself. He had a soft spot for pokers in his day, nothing too violent, but menacing nonetheless. It leant a certain baseness to his own case. The doctors took a dim view of him. Violence was really passé in clinical psychology at this stage in the game, excepting for self-mutilation which guaranteed personal notoriety and care from the best doctors.

'So you're off today then,' Ambrose said again, eyeing Sean's bun.

'Take it,' Sean said. 'What a sweet tooth you have, Ambrose.'

Ambrose obliged himself. 'It all began with a sweet tooth, Sean,' Ambrose smiled.

'What are you talking about?' Sean didn't wait for the answer. 'I don't know if I can face them back at the university,' Sean whispered, leaning over the bun.

Ambrose pulled the bun toward himself. 'And why's that?'

Sean took a few crumbs and put them on his head for the finch. 'Nobody believes that anyone recovers from a breakdown.'

'It only matters what you think,' Ambrose answered in a perfunctory manner. He licked the bun to end a pause and break eye contact. 'And sure, you can't lose your job. You're tethered, aren't you?'

'Tenured, Ambrose. It's tenured,' Sean said, nodding his head.

'Do you know what I was in for?' Sean said.

Ambrose put the bun down and swallowed. 'It's all behind you.' He felt sorry for Sean. From what Ambrose gathered, he had given a lecture on the meaninglessness of God, then went down to his former primary school, and hit an old nun he'd borne a grudge against for forty-odd years. They had that much in common, a penchant for hurting old ladies, a couple of Granny Bashers.

'I should have killed her. On principle alone,' Sean burst out laughing. 'She was a real old cunt.'

'You're a desperate bastard,' Ambrose smiled.

'I don't think they give a damn about me here,' Sean said, touching Ambrose's hand. 'They thought it was some sexual perversion, some sort of connection between nuns and sex.'

'A bad habit,' Ambrose grinned.

'That's it now, Ambrose. You get no respect unless you're a pervert in this world.' Sean smiled again. 'I told them I had four children by my wife and that there was never a moment of equivocation in our whole marriage. I told them I was a perfect specimen of manliness. I have a pair of balls here that would be the envy of many a donkey. And I rowed for the university. Did you know that, Ambrose? I've got all sorts of cups. Do you want to see them?'

'Keep your balls to yourself. I'll take your word on both counts, Sean.' Ambrose raised his head as though he was wearing a hat, stopping the neck from going all the way back. 'Well. You're off anyway.'

'I saw your notes upstairs,' Sean said, turning to his tea to change the subject. 'You don't mind that . . . '

Ambrose flushed for an instant, the bun lodged in the back of his throat. 'It's very . . . crude at this stage. Therapy is what they call it. Ah . . . Nothing literary or even approaching fiction.' Ambrose swallowed in agitation.

'That kind of brooding stuff should have a black cat in it,' Sean answered in earnest. 'If you want, I'll look it over for you when you have things sorted out. I've taught all the great existentialist works. You know Camus' novel, *The Stranger*, which starts with the man who says, "Mother died today, or was it yesterday. I can't be sure." You might like that one, Ambrose.'

'A black cat,' Ambrose grinned. 'By God. Now why didn't I think of that?' There was no point in striking Sean at this stage; he was on the way out. But Jesus, Ambrose felt pushed to his limit with that one. 'Where would you put what I have in the scope of literature?' Ambrose said.

The self-consciousness of his question was evident to Sean who smiled feebly. 'Well it's early yet, but I could see you working toward a good skit about the cat driving the protagonist insane. People have that sort of fascination with cats.' Sean smiled at Ambrose. 'The cat would be a real topper.'

Ambrose looked at him, his fist tense, filling with blood. 'Do you think I can't handle anything beyond some feline caper?'

'Of course not, Ambrose. I can see now that I've put you off. The cat is just a metaphor, Ambrose. Don't take me wrong now, ol' friend.'

The will to talk left Ambrose again. These were the moments when nothing could be communicated. It was better to let the fury pass into its own pathological playground, into his head where at least he had the comfort of having the last word, which was really what he wanted in the end, the ability to start and to finish something.

Sean drank his tea in silence, his weak eyes pleading for forgiveness. He tried to say something once or twice, opening his mouth. But nothing came, only the smell of the sweet tea. After a quarter of an hour Sean managed, 'Would you do me a favour?' He drained the rest of his tea.

'All right,' Ambrose said, his finger scanning the table for crumbs, making a clicking sound to get the bird's attention.

'When they come, could you . . . not be around?' The tips of his ears turned red.

Ambrose felt a twinge of pain stab him in the temples. He wasn't good enough for the likes of Sean's people, but he nodded anyway in an obliging manner. 'I'll stay away.'

The finch swooped down and landed on Sean's hand. 'I can see now that you have it in for me, Ambrose.'

Ambrose shook his head, looking away from Sean. He would have got up, but his legs resisted.

Sean's hand trembled so much that the finch flew back into the ceiling.

'I think it might rain,' Ambrose said, looking up at the sky overhead and shivered.

Ambrose Takes Times Off
to stand in the long hallway as Sean and his people leave the institution.

Back in his bedroom after Sean had left, Ambrose refused

point-blank to describe it. He had been crying. He read over the words.

I am a sick Limerick man . . . I am an angry Limerick man. I am an unattractive Limerick man, in the aftermath of World War Two . . .

He'd been told to use the first person voice, but he resisted on the grounds that the evocation of the first person voice was too Protestant, a vulgar evangelism. Ambrose preferred the third person voice, although he began everything in the first person, then turned it into the third person. He liked the intercession of a third person voice, a supplicator repeating his words, a form of confession, the 'I' voice speaking to the intercessor who spoke to God on his behalf and passed forgiveness back again to him. For all his moroseness, his hatred of people, he couldn't be without them. Yes, he nodded his head as if he'd discovered something about himself. He liked annoying other people. It came as a revelation.

Again he read over the words, now with the stuff turned into the third person.

He is a sick Limerick man . . . He is an angry Limerick man. He is an unattractive Limerick man, in the aftermath of World War Two . . .

He nodded his head with satisfaction. The third person was his man all the way on this one. But something was not quite right. He laboured again.

*

He is a sick, angry, unattractive Limerick man living in the aftermath of World War Two . . .

But there was still something amiss. Was it the impersonal tone of the third person, detached, no name, and the present tense usage which seemed to set everything off-kilter? The third person belongs to the past for some reason, once a character is conceived and set into motion he necessarily must be followed, his story unfolds as a chronicle, the action is contemplated not really as it happens, but after it has happened, for in the act of acknowledging and documenting one action, the character has moved on a step or two into the future. The character always occupies a slim range of freedom where his actions cannot be anticipated, they must be seen, recognized, and then written . . . Take for instance what will be said next, that is, the next word in this story . . . Not even Ambrose knows, or he is not conscious of it until it is written, and even as the pen writes what the head has decided, his idea has become part of a past, the time between thought and action, the slipstream where there is only hard labour, the committing of expression into text, the need and then the fulfillment. And so to begin . . .

Ambrose was a sick, angry, unattractive Limerick man living in the aftermath of World War Two . . .

Ambrose thought of himself as a victim of a terrible lack of self-respect and confidence to put himself up against others. There are those who will say, 'Man is magnificent! This signifies that although I, personally, have not built airplanes, I have the benefit of those particular inventions, and that I personally, being a man, can consider myself responsible for, and honoured by, achievements that are particular to some men. It is to assume that we can ascribe value to man according to the most distinguished deeds of certain men.'

Ambrose would have none of that, a victim of parochialism, a man flung out on the edge of Europe, a loner, he did not want to be implicated in any action other than his own. Or if pressed, and he was now, Ambrose saw himself as a metaphor of a backward nation which had to forego the spectacle of World War Two – for budgetary concerns. A nation which did not participate in the great wars, fighting with itself, no Battle of Britain, no D-Day, no collective horror, no Auschwitz. His national destiny was just plain madness, a state of nationhood associated not with a word like 'Democracy', but with words like, 'Guinness Stout', or, worse still, 'Catholicism'.

The long and short of it was Ambrose could not write the sociological novel of his dreams. Irish life was too alien. It reflected nothing of the sociological nature of the world outside. And what of it? There was always painting or basket weaving at the end of the day if nothing else worked. Outside the world collapsed into a monotonous rain, the pitter patter fingering boredom on the sill bearded in moss. Ambrose heard the bell in the hall outside calling him to lunch, that Pavlov's bell, and dutifully secreted juice into his mouth and stomach. There was so much outside his control.

He traipsed down the cold corridor, meeting other men in ill-fitting suits heading down to lunch and the sudden banter of men bartering food. 'I'll trade you two butters for your rice pudding. What do you say, Frank?'

'And a bowl of cornflakes tomorrow?'

'You must be coddin' me. Two butters for a rice pudding is all you get, Frank.'

Ambrose had his hands in his pockets, dutifully moving forward along the polished hardwood floor.

Downstairs, a nurse with a round face, fat calves and pink fingers asked everyone to show their teeth, checking for cuts or broken teeth, her big fingers running over the gum line. Ambrose stood watching the Foot and Mouth inspection he'd seen his father perform on animals and here he was leaning down to this squat agricultural nurse, showing his teeth in a big horse-like grin. 'And how are we today, Ambrose?'

'Very well, nurse,' Ambrose displayed his yellow teeth.

'You're looking better, Ambrose . . . ' She proceeded along the line, screwing up her face. 'Let me see your gums.'

Ambrose went into the hall, said his prayers and then sat down among the disturbed, the self-conscious and the plain mad. He ate at a slow even pace, his knife and fork in either hand, cutting and selecting pieces of meat and vegetable, the potatoes set off to the side. He swabbed everything in gravy, coveting each mound, predatory, bringing it to his mouth. He kept his eyes closed or squinted as much as possible. The unbearable click of mastication reached its usual pitch, the sputtering attempts at swallowing. Ambrose closed his eyes and mouth. He felt there was nothing as pathetic as a creature who ate with its mouth open.

After that, Ambrose went out to the gazebo and loosened his belt, another meal, another lump of flesh to add to his body. His suit would not last at this rate through the spring. It was already threading at the crotch and under the armpits. He estimated that he had gained nearly a stone inside of five weeks this time around. He settled himself, blowing out his cheeks. It was sunny overhead now that the rain had passed, giving everything a muggy feeling which made him sweat. Ambrose reached into his pocket, took a sprinkle of crumbs and put them on his hand and waited for the finches to come.

Ambrose sleeps in his clothes in his small room, which is the only form of escape that comes to him now.

Sleep evaded him this time round. Soon it would be pills for what should have been natural. His head was at him even in his dreams. He curled up on the first of many lonely nights now that Sean was gone. There was nobody to lull him to sleep. He'd always had brothers in bed with him, the feeling of warmth at his back. The dreams were of a particular sort, 'literary dreams' Ambrose called them, induced by the free time he had to read at the library in the hospital. Why did they have a library in a hospital?

Beckett was occupying prominence in Ambrose's head these days, probably because he was still alive somewhere. Ambrose often shut one of Beckett's books and wondered what the hell he must have been up to over in France. Once his eyelids drooped in sleep, up went the curtain and there he was, Beckett lurking in his mind, that old cunt. It was the old Beckett he always envisioned, the wrinkled lunatic with the chiselled face and shock of white hair. Beckett was, if not shy, then irascible.

'What are you doing here?' Ambrose shouted.

Beckett let a shard of light cut down the left angle of his face. 'I'm waiting,' he whispered.

'Waiting for what?' Ambrose shouted.

'Waiting for Godot.'

231

Ambrose's expression soured. He had walked himself into that one. 'Well fuck off with yourself,' Ambrose shouted out again. The conversation really ended at this point every night. Ambrose was not versed enough in Beckett to ask a question, and Beckett was laconic at the best of times, or he spoke French, much to Ambrose's chagrin.

To have fixated on the likes of Beckett was beyond Ambrose's understanding. The great myth of Irish misanthropy had set up shop in his head. Now it sought some historical justification. If he could not talk about World War Two, then what the hell did he have to say about anything in this world? 'Yes, you see Dad was a pig slaughterer down in Munster Meats during the time when men were killing men all over the world . . . ' No, he was stuck with misanthropy, a poor man's version of horror. The economy of Irish lunacy could be traced to a banjaxed system of government. Nothing had ever worked in the country. This misanthropy dated back to Swift and *Gulliver's Travels*. It wasn't a child's story at all. Ambrose had read that somewhere in the library. He didn't like to keep track of references, and the more he repeated something he'd read, the more he forgot that he'd read it and felt he must have said it himself. That would have accounted for the *Notes From Underground*.

Beckett coughed and tapped Ambrose on the arm and said, as though in mid-thought, 'And if I speak of principles, when there are none, I can't help it, there must be some somewhere.'

Ambrose came back with his own one. 'We are the only creatures who define things by what they are not.' Ambrose beamed. 'How's that for you?'

'But it doesn't get to your point, now does it Ambrose?'

'I have no point,' Ambrose answered. 'That's the point, you see, no point.'

Even Beckett winced. He picked up Ambrose's manuscript, the bit that was on the table beside the bottle of Lucozade. 'You cannot mention everything in its proper place, you must choose, between the things not worth mentioning and those even less so. For if you set out to mention everything you would never be done, and that's what counts, to be done, to have done.'

'To be or not to be!' Ambrose shouted. 'Is that what you're talking about?'

'Oh, if it were only that simple,' Beckett whispered.

'I want to set things straight with my mother!' Ambrose shouted. 'That's all I really want!'

'It's the beginning that has you now, finding the origin of what is now in motion, to spin something back on itself without referencing the knowledge of what has proceeded. What you need is to forget the concept and remember only the details in order, without bias. Just tell it straight.'

Ambrose drank from the bottle of Lucozade, sitting amid the darkness of the room, his feet unseen on the floor.

'If I could give you a word of advice,' Beckett sighed. 'I began at the beginning, like an old ballocks, can you imagine that? Here's my beginning . . . I took a lot of trouble with it. Here it is. It gave me a lot of trouble. It was the beginning, do you understand? Whereas now it's nearly the end. Is what I do now any better? I don't know. That's beside the point. Here's my beginning.'

Ambrose pulled at his own jaded face, the loosening expression of his skin animating a caricature of his former youth. 'I've heard that one before. Will I tell you a story about Jack O'Nory? Will I begin it? That's all that's in it!'

'You're catching on,' Beckett conceded. 'But the element of despair is lacking.'

Ambrose got up and turned on the light in the room.

'Turn that light off,' a voice called down the hall. An orderly came with keys on a ring and rapped on the door. 'Turn that light off in there!'

Ambrose obeyed and stood over by the window, seeking the invisible moon. He listened for the steps, counting the fourteen steps that took the orderly back to his desk.

Beckett was there in the darkness. 'I began again,' he whispered. 'I began again. But little by little with a different aim, no longer in order to succeed, but in order to fail . . . '

Ambrose found tears in his eyes. 'Will you leave me alone?' Ambrose wiped his eyes. The con that had been pulled on the poor and uneducated out in those lonesome houses in constant darkness. Lack of light translated into a psychosis of vacuity, and not translated into the sheer economic tyranny of those who had nothing, the polemic of the poor, robbed by a psychology of nothingness, a debunked Marxism, 'Workers of the world, don't give a shite!'

Beckett whispered in the background, 'For to know nothing is nothing, not to want to know anything likewise, but to be beyond knowing, to know you are beyond knowing anything, that is when peace enters in, to the soul of the incurious seeker.'

Reading had contaminated Ambrose. What to do with Beckett, expatriate of Ireland and his language, burning bridges as he digressed, bilingual ballocks, defining nothingness in two languages, fuckin show off . . . Where to begin after the opening of Murphy, 'The sun shone, having no alternative, on the nothing new.' Ambrose was still at the old sherbet horizon, a sunrise that smears the sky with afterbirth of newness, etc. Suicide still had its appeal for Ambrose, but sure it had already been done. And for that matter, so had death. 'To know that you are beyond knowing anything . . .' Where the hell was there ever an impassive incurious seeker? Ambrose was unwilling to believe there existed such a man outside of fiction. How that Beckett stuff passed into the hands of the youth galled Ambrose. How about the insult to the poor misfortunes in those dark Beckett places who were deprived of their humanity, so that now when literary people go down to the country for the holidays and see those types, they rush them and begin to ask them questions about form and content, about the peace that has entered into the heart of their incurious search. Oh lamentable old men in black suits and dingy shirts sipping pints and nodding or winking, or just nodding and winking, infinitely patient to persistent questions. 'Sir, is it true that you have equally distributed in your pockets sixteen sucking stones?' Jasus, the poor bastards can't milk a cow without being pestered off the face of the earth. No wonder they are confined to their houses like celebrities who must hide from the public. Yes, Beckett, you old bastard, you've ruined the peace of our aging population of farmers, sipping your chilled continental wine on a sun-drenched Parisian outdoor café, eating cubes of cheese and thinking about body-warm porter set beside salted potatoes, a historical leap of national consciousness. The incongruity of wine sipped, not poured into the throat, a delicacy of intent and pretension, a Jesus drink, turning water into wine, the slow attentuated movement . . . What could be more different than the Parisian wine pucker to the Irish porter yawn?

Ambrose takes a bible and swears he will not read another printed word that is not his own until he has said what has to be said.

But, Jesus, what do you do when you have a Nobel prize winner staring you in the face night after night? And, more to the point, what was Beckett doing here in Ambrose's story? How he got on this kick was all mystery. Ambrose wanted to say big things. He looked to Europe with envy. At least they had something to feel truly guilty about. They were left with narrative plot, with graves, things that did not have to be dredged out of a solipsistic mind. There was poetry in genocide. Ambrose felt that hating one's mother couldn't be the source of life's great mystery, it was shameless, no, down-right immoral, to have climax centre around an unfortunate incident with a poker.

Ambrose hasn't given up on himself yet. His mother is going to get what's coming to her if it kills him into the bargain.

Ambrose felt it slipping away before he even began. He made a clicking sound with his tongue. At first, he couldn't say his name and place of birth, and then he made up some sort of national psychosynthesis, and a bad job at that. It was all drivel. Maybe he could begin again, change a few names, but keep the material in the main. To ride a bicycle one needs to get momentum.
    Ambrose felt that two-thirds of anything good was plagiarism. To quote yet again another eminent Irishman, 'The

entire corpus of existing literature should be regarded as a limbo from which discerning authors could draw their characters as required . . . The modern novel should be largely a work of reference.' With that at least he could save the beginning without having to resort to probability. It became an issue of prowess, of his erudite nature. People would have to say at least, 'Christ, he's well read anyway.'

Ambrose looked back over what he'd said to this point. It was a long way from Clare to here. Not a word about his mother, that fuckin poxy ol' whore, the source of his misery and blight. He was fuming with himself, pinching himself, biting the lining of his mouth. He opened the window in his small room and stood at attention and roared.

Of course, he blamed it on the place he was born in. Imagine being born a Limerick man, a literary heritage of dirty rhyming, the scope of literature honed down to five sing-song lines. Jasus Christ. At least Shakespeare had fourteen. A Limerick! What literary precedent: There once was a man from Nantucket . . .

It was all there. The relatives coming in and out to see him. He could do a lot with the finch, the anticipation of the eggs hatching, rebirth, soft wings fanning the air above his head, everything dripping with Catholic metaphor: Ambrose is visited by the Holy Ghost. Ambrose's ascension into Heaven. Or Sean could ring Ambrose up and ask about the finch, and it would be believable. Throw in the black cat for gravy. Sean had said it himself. Mankind has a soft spot for animals. It could sell books.

It was weeks later that Ambrose felt he had his man. For all the significance of Sarsfield and his Wild Geese, Ambrose knew he was on his own. It would be a hard job to get anybody interested in 1691. What he needed was something to connect his father's hard years with the pigs, his own wasted years in the Civil Service, his amorphous thesis on the failure of Capitalism in the late twentieth century, and lastly the fanaticism of his mother and her religion. It was a tall order, even for a lunatic.

One day in the library, while reading the lives of saints, Ambrose came across a reference to his mother's favourite saint. She'd been a bag of bones robbed from a grave by a priest, pure invention. St Philomena had been kicked out of Heaven. Ambrose couldn't believe it. His mother, that sanctimonious old bitch, was in violation of Church doctrine, praying to her statue of a banned saint. He copied verbatim.

In 1802, in the cemetery of St Priscilla, an ancient tomb, upon which was inscribed 'Lumena – Paxte – Cum Fi,' was unearthed. Nearby was a phial thought to contain blood. The inscription was reconstructed to read 'Pax – Tecum – Filumena,' and the bones were accepted as those of a young virgin martyr of the 3rd century. Don Francesco di Lucia, the parish priest of Mugnano del Cardinale, near Naples, transferred these relics to the place of honour in his church and wrote a life of Philomena based upon dubious visions and his own imagination. However, there is no hagiographical or liturgical evidence for Philomena's existence before di Lucia's imaginative account. On April 18, 1961, the Congregation of Rites struck Philomena's name from the list of saints for lack of historical evidence.

Ambrose signed the letter, 'Anonymous', licked the envelope

and posted it. He'd never felt more liberated in all his life. He had his unequivocal evidence, not just psychosis.

The library served a great function in his time of need. Another day he was reading some old newspapers when he came across . . . 'I wear a brick on my shoulder to show the house I come from . . . ' I have been characterized as 'a lineal descendant of the impertinent thief; Judas Iscariot . . . ' What the hell was this, anti-Semitism in Limerick? Ambrose bunched up his trousers at the knee and let his legs shake as he read. A certain Father Creagh of the Redemptorists in 1904 had given a sermon condemning the usury of the Jews in Limerick, whom he called 'leeches, living off the poor, of being enemies of Catholicism . . . ' Ambrose licked his lips. All great fiction must have the eternal Jew wandering in it somewhere. The Jews had been accused of lending money to the poor at exorbitant rates. Father Creagh had led a boycott of the Jews, and set about righting the wrongs in a practical way: 1) Establishing a drapery store in Parnell Street 2) Establishing a shirt factory in Hartstonge Street 3) Founding a savings bank attached to the Confraternity.

There were, of course, incidents of violence associated with the struggle that eventually drove the Jews out of Limerick in what became known as the Limerick Pogrom.

Now, the deciding issue remained. Was Father Creagh an anti-Semite or was the entire episode motivated by economic hardship? Still, Ambrose wasn't a man for the particulars. The fact that something happened at all thrilled him. He found another quote from the *United Irishman*, praising Creagh for pointing out 'the Jews . . . for what they are – nine-tenths of them – usurers and parasites . . . '

To Ambrose's way of thinking, the whole thing had the

makings of a great story, the Jews in the Capital City of Bacon, the impropriety of Jews standing by as the town went around with the dirty pig meat slaughtered and carried in dripping bloody newspaper wrappings, the Jews watching the Pork Butcher's annual mass. The possibility got him going, the bewildering spectacle of the 'Wandering Jew in the City of Bacon'. That was at least a beginning, a title, and hadn't he been long enough with everything else, to have this fall into his lap, only justice for the strife of his former months.

Oh, when it rains, it pours. Ambrose fell upon another story one evening down at the library, drinking tea and eating digestives. In 1919, at the beginning of the troubles with the IRA and the British Army, the British decided that the workers crossing the Shannon to their work would have to have a pass. The workers refused and began a strike. Then all of a sudden the workers decided to send off a telegram to Lenin over in Moscow, declaring themselves a Soviet Republic, the first outside Russia, asking for help. The siege mentality had never left Limerick. They were always ready to withdraw into themselves, into enclaves of cloven-hoofed trotters and their masters, wishing for a former glory. They issued new money and ration cards and began preparing a constitution . . . Ambrose imagined something like, 'This little piggy went to market, as it was a democracy . . . This little piggy bought bread and butter, because it was a capitalist society . . . ' such shite he'd never heard the like of before. The fledgling satellite lasted for ten days. The bishops called the whole thing, 'the work of Satan'. The Army was called in to surround the place and that ended that, 'The Communist Satellite Republic in the City of Bacon.'

Ambrose scribbled all of it down furiously, the cataloguing

of historical fact. Whatever his story would be, it was to be sociological and not psychological. Ambrose wanted that established right from the beginning. Because you write from an asylum does not mean that everything is psychological.

Ambrose is interrupted and told it is time for his appointment with his doctor.

Some kind of guilt kept Ambrose buttoned up. His doctor put it another way. He said to Ambrose, 'Any system, living or nonliving, tends to disorder, to change in such a way as to minimize its energy content, that is, its ability to do work. You understand Ambrose, don't you?' He pointed to Ambrose's shaking knees. 'Entropy, Ambrose, are you with me? You must let go of guilt and move toward entropy.'

'Entropy. You mean like the Civil Service,' Ambrose said, smiling. Then he stiffened his shaking legs. 'Guilt is a scientific principle, potential energy, is that what we've come to, Doctor?' Ambrose went on, feigning enlightenment. He was going to get his money's worth from the science that had been forced down him at school.

The doctor let his tongue scan his teeth. 'As you move toward that death, you will either produce a byproduct of importance or not.' The doctor stopped for a moment and then said, 'Well, let me put it another way. Guilt is a scientific principle, Ambrose.' The doctor scrawled the words down in his notebook.

Ambrose was flabbergasted. He could see the doctor was the kind who would rob a gold watch off a corpse. Now he saw the importance of copyright.

'How's the book coming?' The doctor smiled.

241

'To tell the truth, I didn't know where to begin,' Ambrose said.

'That's very postmodern,' The doctor smiled.

'Tripe.' Ambrose rubbed his chin. His tongue hung between his teeth. 'I'm going to start at the beginning,' he said at last.

'That's very Freudian,' The doctor smiled.

'Call it what you will, it's all I know.'

'So, what's this that the nurses found in your room?' the doctor said, looking up, holding a notebook.

'That's nothing,' Ambrose shouted. 'You have no right to go through my things.'

The doctor licked his index finger and smiled. 'Let's see now what do we have here? Ah yes . . . "Christmas didn't just come; it had to be planned or it would be a disaster . . . "'